User Pays

Wendy Howitt

Wendy Howitt is the author of two young adult books, USER PAYS and BULLETPROOF. She has written on staff for Vogue Australia, Harper's Bazaar and the Sydney Morning Herald. As a freelancer, her byline has appeared in many publications, including Cleo, Inside Out magazine and The Australian Magazine. She has also won two beauty journalism awards.

Chapter 1

"What are you doing in there?"

"Nothing. Go away."

"Are you sulking because Mum said you couldn't have a new iPhone cover?"

"No."

"Then open the door."

"No."

It was 4pm on Thursday. I was lying sideways on the bed in my room with the door firmly closed against my nosy 10-year-old sister, who lay on the floor on the other side of it. I could hear her adenoidal breathing through the gap under the door. I knew what that meant. Any minute now she would be barging in. That's because my sister has no personal boundaries whatsoever – yet another of my crosses to bear.

Scuffle. The door handle rattled. I looked upside down around my room for a weapon. Nothing hard was at hand so I stretched for my 1D memorabilia cushion and waited for the myopic brown eye that would be soon be peering through the crack. There. Whoosh. Missed. Damn.

And there she was: my sister, who had the proportions of Angelina Ballerina, pirouetting into my private space.

I sat up. "Get out."

"No."

"What's the rule?"

"Closed Door. No Entry." Milly didn't look at me as she spoke. It was a resented rule.

"So? What are you still doing here?"

Milly extended a pointed toe, bent and twiddled with my silver dog ring holder. "I just want to make sure you're okay."

I fell back on the bed. "I'm okay. Now please just go."

Milly lifted up my aqua handled hairbrush and twirled it in the air. "So, you're not mad at me?"

"Nope. Put that down." My eyes narrowed. "Why?"

"Nothing." She put down the brush and nonchalantly stroked my silver dolphin pendant on black cord.

I sighed. "What did you do?"

"I didn't do anything … It was Ms Patrina. I was only going to wear it during warm-up." "It" turned out to be my favourite black jumper. Milly's ballet teacher had confiscated it for not being regulation pink. "But I'll get it back. Pinky promise."

It wasn't the first time Milly had borrowed my things and, for the millionth time, I wished I could put a padlock on my door. Or, even better, move into my own apartment. As if that was going to happen. I couldn't even afford a new cover for my phone.

You're probably thinking I sound like just another 15-year-old girl obsessed with privacy and her iPhone. But until this year, I didn't even have a phone. I was living in the middle of whoop-whoop on the west coast of Australia being home-schooled by my mother who was a teacher. Though we were originally from Sydney, we'd moved to the middle of nowhere three years ago when my dad, a geologist, got a job working for a mining magnate. Apart from Milly's light fingers, it wasn't so bad. We had Skype. I also got to rescue a lot of native animals which was really cool.

At the end of last year, everything changed. First, my dad lost his job and we had to move back to Sydney. We couldn't go back to our old house because we'd sold that so we ended up in a derelict rental with the landlord from hell. On the upside, I got accepted into this great school on a part scholarship. To celebrate, my parents bought me an iPhone.

"It's not the latest model, honey, but it's got all the bells and whistles just like all you girls need," said my dad.

One minute I was dressed in shorts on the verandah listening to tame magpies, summarising six chapters of *To Kill a Mockingbird* and answering questions about its main themes – prejudice, racism and loss of innocence – and reciting the reasons for the Vietnam War for history, the next I was dressed in a regulation knee-length uniform attending Northcote Grammar School for Girls with a data plan and about a zillion school rules to remember.

All of this I could handle.

It was the girls themselves that had me freaked. Or, more specifically, a group of girls whose behaviour in the playground was nothing like I'd encountered before. It was like being dropped in a foreign country with a new language and customs to learn and I'd brought along the wrong guide book. I hated that feeling: of not being prepared. If it wasn't for Brigitte, I don't know what I would have done.

Brigitte Riley had been my best friend in kindergarten. We'd met in the sandpit. Brigitte made the best mud pies back then. I was her best customer. We stayed in touch when I moved away and she was the first person I told when I found out we were coming back and I'd gotten in to Northcote Grammar School for Girls. She was ecstatic. She'd been there since Year 7.

On my first day, she met me on the corner of my street and Trafalgar Road and we walked to school together. She'd also gotten me a job with her at the local golf club where we were paid the minimum wage by Brigitte's aunt, the club's social secretary, to hand around food on sticks to new members. We spent most Sunday nights watching *Doctor Who*. Recently, her mum had invited me to see *Guys and Dolls* with them for Brigitte's 16th birthday which was in a few months. Brigitte had always been into musicals. I'd said yes even though I wasn't.

It still didn't help. Nothing helped. Not even crying on my bed after school which is what I had been doing this afternoon when Milly barged in pretending to be starring in *Dance Academy*.

My bedroom door opened up again. Mum. It was ballet time and she was looking for Milly.

"Great," I said. "Everyone come in. Please."

Mum squinted at me.

"Have you been crying?"

"No! I just want to be left alone."

Mum frowned. "Is this about your phone cover?"

"No! Yes. I don't see why I can't get a new one?" All the girls at school had these cool covers that resembled wooden tablets. Mine was fluoro and sparkled so much Milly coveted it – I rest my case.

"This is so unlike you." Mum began to pick up clothes from my floor, folding them and putting them away. Then I saw her expression change. Oh no. I knew that look. It meant she was going to give me a pep talk. I had to stop her.

"Mum. It's nothing. I'm fine."

She sat down on the bed anyway.

"Going to school after three years of being home-schooled with your sister is a huge adjustment. You're feeling anxious. I completely understand that. It's okay to be scared and overwhelmed. But you're going to be fine. You're a smart, strong and beautiful person, inside and out. All the girls will soon see that."

"Yes, I know. You've told me this, like, a million times. It's not even about that."

"Ah. A boy …"

I could almost see the synapses firing inside Mum's brain as she latched on to her second favourite topic: my hormones.

"Muum."

"… Well, of course this is all completely natural what you're feeling … you are nearly 16, after all, and …" she was off. It was so embarrassing. I fell back on the bed.

Since coming to Sydney, I had totally become obsessed with boys but I didn't want to discuss it with my mother. I just wanted a new iPhone cover.

"If it's that important to you to feel like you fit in, you can have it …"

Huh? Since when did we switch back to phone covers? I sat up.

"It is. It *really* is."

"Not too expensive, though. Until dad gets a new job and I stop being a substitute, money's tight."

"Thank you, thank you, *thank you*."

I hugged her hard. She smiled.

"I can drop you at the shopping centre when I take Milly to ballet. But you've got to get ready now" – I nodded and opened my mouth, but Mum interrupted – "I know, you were born ready. Just like your dad. Could you buy some milk? Oh, and you'll have to catch the bus home. I can't wait. I have to collect Gert."

I quickly brushed my hair – you never knew what boys might be lurking at the shops – and put on my dolphin necklace. It had been a present from Aunt Gert for my last birthday. I loved it. Gert was my father's great aunt and, at 90, she was ancient. She lived in a hermetically-sealed old people's home and every week she'd have dinner at our place. Tonight, it was soup on account of Aunt Gert's ill-fitting dentures. She was also a stickler for punctuality so Mum practically burned rubber as she left us at the entrance of the community hall, next door to the shops, and the place where Ms Patrina vainly attempted to turn a leotard-clad elephant called Milly into a graceful ballerina.

I winced at the squeaky music coming through the open window of the community hall. Thank God the bus stop was far away on the other side of the shopping centre.

I bought a container of milk and the phone cover. I put it on straightaway, stroking the smooth wood finish, then headed inside the splendour of our local pharmacy to test fragrances and one lip gloss after another in stripes on the inside of my wrist. I knew it was time to go when the salesperson began to hover. I dabbed the winner – *Pink Kisses* – on my lips, grabbed the bag containing the milk and headed to the bus stop.

As I stared at my phone trying to figure out what bus to catch, I heard a popping sound. Slowly, I became aware of a sweet scent with which I'd just become familiar: Vera Wang *Princess*. In the pharmacy, it smelled beautiful and exotic and full of promise – and came with a whopping $89 price tag. Out there in the afternoon sun and low hum of traffic, it was like being transported to another world.

I looked up to discover its source. A girl wearing a cap and one of those shorty jumpsuits that I wasn't allowed but coveted stood beside me, pulling at a wad of lurid pink bubble gum from her mouth and blowing on it before returning it. It was Natasha Fielding, one of the popular girls in my year at school. I was about to say hi, then remembered that she hadn't spoken to me all term even though we were in the same English class. I ducked my head back to my bus app and did my best to ignore her even though all I could hear was her snapping gum between sighs. When she eventually spoke, I assumed she wasn't talking to me.

"God, I hate public transport." A pause. Then, "Tell me you agree."

I glanced up in surprise and saw her looking at me.

"What? Sorry? Were you talking to me?"

She chewed slowly and rather thoughtfully, not answering me straightaway. After what felt like forever, but was probably only a second or two, she seemed to come to a decision.

"You're the new girl at school, aren't you?" she said, giving me an encouraging smile.

I nodded, "Yes, I'm Lucy."

"I'm Natasha. Welcome to our school." I didn't bother to correct her that, technically, I was no longer new; that term one was nearly over. I was just pleased, I guess, that she had noticed me. She kept talking, like we were already friends. She had been at the shops, too, with her mum. But her mum had left her there, barefoot, in the car park, and she hadn't a clue why.

"She's basically crazy." She twirled her forefinger around her ear in the universal gesture for kooky and blew an enormous bubble, practically the size of a balloon. She held it like that for a while and then sucked the sweet air back into her mouth. She chewed again, more grimly this time.

"There's no way I'm getting on a bus. No way. I'm ringing my dad. He's mad at me for getting a D for maths, but he'll pick me up." She sounded confident. "He's going to freak when he hears how Mum abandoned me. *Again*." She stretched the word out to emphasise her point, then stepped closer, looking at the dolphin around my neck. "Nice necklace."

She adjusted her cap so that her hair fell in a ponytail through the gap in the back. She was close enough that I could smell her shampoo beneath the Vera Wang fragrance. She smiled brightly into the afternoon sun.

"He can give you a lift. If you want," and, without waiting for my answer, hit her dad's number.

With a satisfied air, she hung up. "He's coming," and she adjusted her bag with flowered handles and tugged the bubble gum from her mouth, rolling it around in her fingertips while she searched for a bin. There was one about 20 metres away. I watched her closely as she headed for it. Two boys, thongs clamped on dirty feet and blond hair crusty with salt, whistled loudly as they skateboarded past. She wriggled her shoulder in acknowledgement of the compliment, but didn't glance their way. What had she got that I hadn't?

The answer was simple. *Everything.* Her legs were tanned to a golden brown, her toenails were painted a lush strawberry red and her eyes were rimmed in dark green kohl.

When she returned, she took out a sample-sized bottle of perfume and gave herself a spritz. "Want some? Hold out your wrist."

I did as I was told and she squirted me, too.

"Snap." She'd noticed the candy-coloured stripes of lipgloss on my wrist. She held out her own which was striped just like mine. I breathed in the fruity fragrance and thought that maybe we weren't so different, after all. Natasha held out the bottle.

"Here, take it."

I stared at her. "Really?"

What was the catch? But there was none. She was just being generous. She pushed the bottle into my hand.

"Have it. I've got another one at home. Here's Dad."

A shiny black Mercedes pulled in. A man stuck his bald pate out of the rolled-down driver's window like a hound in the breeze and said, "Hi, princess." She grabbed for the door handle but missed when the car skipped forward. He grinned, enjoying his prank. She tried again to open the door. And, again, the car rolled forward, just an inch, but enough to throw her off balance.

"Stop it, Dad! Just let us in."

"Sure thing," but, again, her dad tapped the accelerator. Natasha had had enough. She stamped her foot. I stood still, pop-eyed.

"I wish I'd caught the bus now." She yanked so fiercely at the moving door, her bag slid off her arm, the contents spilling out: a hairbrush, a bunch of lip gloss pots and several packets of gum.

"Fuck," she said, scrambling to pick everything up.

"What did you just say?" her dad said, raising his eyebrows.

"Nothing. I said 'fruit'." Natasha rearranged her bag, herself and her visor.

"Just get in the car," he said suddenly as if he'd lost interest in the prank and all of it.

She got in.

"I should go," I said.

Natasha leaned out, "No, wait. Dad'll give you a lift."

I tentatively put a foot towards the car, half expecting Mr Fielding to take off. But he didn't.

"What star sign are you?" she said to me as I climbed into the scruffy back seat after her.

"Um, Cancer." I collapsed on the leather that stuck a bit to my thighs and, after slipping the perfume sample she'd given me inside my bag, shoved it between my knees.

"I thought you were spending the afternoon shopping with your mother." Mr Fielding ground the car into gear.

"She had a caftan crisis or something and had to run."

"Typical." He started whistling *Born to Run*, glancing back in the rearview mirror. "I haven't met you before, have I?"

"That's because she's new. She's the Scholarship Girl." Natasha made it sound exotic, rather than desperate.

"Hi, Mr Fielding," I said. "Thanks for giving me a lift."

"Do you like the Boss, Lucy? You'd better, if you want a lift home."

"Um, yes. He's great," I said as convincingly as I could.

He nodded his approval.

"Dad's a Leo and he's into Springsteen," said Natasha. "I'm Scorpio."

I couldn't think of anything more to say so lapsed into silence. The Boss played on.

"See you Monday," I called after the brake lights as Mr Fielding's Mercedes disappeared down the hill. I stood for a minute on the driveway, my bag with the milk, my faux-wood phone cover and a little bottle of fragrance slung over my shoulder, the new girl in town who did extra homework and believed in climate change staring at the place where I'd last seen Natasha Fielding.

As I sniffed my wrist again, I noticed the time on the phone in my hand. It was five o'clock. I had been in Natasha's orbit for approximately 20 minutes and already I felt different. I felt special. I breathed in the exotic base notes of the fragrance that Natasha had given me. Was it really only ten hours since I got up and ate my usual breakfast and lived my usual boring life?

Now I'd met Natasha, all that was about to change. I thought about the way the boys openly stared at her, at her long legs and golden hair. I closed my eyes and inhaled once again and thought of how she'd given me her perfume *and* a lift home. I was on the brink of something momentous. I was sure of it, and I was ready.

Chapter 2

In the afternoon of the following day, a frisson of excitement began to build as it always did on Fridays at this school. Fridays marked the beginning of the weekend and after lunch most girls began to whisper in a restless way about how they planned to relax from 3pm onwards and what they'd wear while doing it. As I exchanged my science books for English at my locker, I overheard a couple of girls from the popular group discussing the upcoming night at the oval.

"What's our position on getting there early?"

"No way. We have to be late. It's ..." The blonde girl who was speaking noticed that I was listening. She turned her shoulder and lowered her voice to a whisper so I could no longer hear her. Nursing an armful of books, I shrugged and thought, *Whatever.*

I had never been to an oval gathering, but I'd heard about them. Neither had Brigitte when I asked her about it as we packed up our backpacks at the end of the day.

"Want to go? Could be fun."

I was keen to see what all the fuss was about.

Brigitte pulled a face. "Why would you want to go to a place with overflowing garbage bins, misspelled graffiti on the toilet block walls and a field where nobody believes in picking up after their dogs, and hang out with a bunch of wasted people?"

Brigitte, who always met her mum after school on Fridays because she had swimming squads, left me with a wave.

* * *

"I wonder what happened last night?"

It was Saturday night and Brigitte and I were arranging sprigs of plastic foliage around platters of sushi and re-heated sausage rolls in the kitchen of Northcote Golf Club.

"I aced my flips," said Brigitte.

Huh?

"Last night at training, my coach told me my flips were getting better."

"That's great, Brig. But, umm, actually I was meaning the oval."

Brigitte extended the kitchen tap to make a hose and turned it onto a pile of lipstick-stained glasses.

"I can't believe you're still on about that."

As well as handing around food, we had to collect the dirty glasses and wash them up. Tonight, the women were decked out in silk sheaths and diamante stilettos and the men wore open-collared shirts. Together they guzzled brightly-coloured drinks loaded with ice, frothy beer or cask riesling that Scott Morgan, the barman, decanted into fancy carafes. Outside, by the pond on the terrace, grown men wearing napkins for party hats were trying to catch goldfish with clumsy hands until Scott went out and told them it was against the rules. I wondered if Scott ever went to oval parties.

Brigitte went out, ostensibly to fetch more used glasses, but really to see her uncle in action. When he got drunk he danced the Nutbush. She came into the kitchen with her eyes nearly popping out of her head.

"I just saw Mr Hargraves kissing Deborah up against one of the ladies' lockers."

"Are you sure it was Mr Hargraves and not Scott?"

Mr Hargraves was the happily married local real estate agent with three kids under four; Deborah was a waitress with thin eyebrows, long calves that we called 'cankles' behind her back, and a soft spot for Scott, who was 18 and hot.

Brigitte threw me a hurt look. I'd forgotten she had a total crush on Scott. She made us spend hours discussing his finer points (not many, in my view, apart from the fact he was very, very good looking). He, on the other hand, didn't even know our names, despite having worked with us both since Christmas. Brigitte didn't let that bother her. She believed that her love would conquer all.

"Sorry, course it wouldn't be Scott," I hastily reassured her. I picked up the tray, "This I've got to see," and put my back against the swinging door that separated the kitchen from the velveteen splendour that was the golf club dining room and was nearly run over by Scott, a tray of middy glasses held aloft by his sinewy tanned arms.

"Get out of the way, Linda. How many times do I have to tell you? Where's your friend? She's gotta wash these fast." I winced at his dismissive tone but meekly stepped aside to let him through.

"Are you sure it's love you feel for Scott, not lust?" I asked Brigitte while she was at the sink, madly washing glasses.

"Love, definitely."

I wasn't sure if I knew the difference. And how would I find out? I didn't even know any boys, let alone one who would be into me enough to find out. If only I was willowy and blonde and eye-catching, like Natasha.

"Did you see the way Scott put the empties next to the sink? He's so thoughtful," sighed Brigitte. The shift was over and we stood outside, yawning on the flagged driveway at the end of our shift, waiting for Brigitte's dad to pick us up, our 10 dollar bills folded up tightly in the back pockets of our skinny jeans.

"I heard him call you Bridg," I said. Actually, he was telling her to move out of the way of the fridge but she was my best friend and deserved a little happiness.

"It's awesome having you at school with me," said Brigitte. "Just like old times. Some of the girls are stuck up, but our group isn't."

"Nope," I said, hugging her. "They're lovely. I love your friends." And I did.

It was just that they had different interests. But I didn't tell Brigitte that.

Scott ran down the stairs, whistling between his teeth; his clip-on tie in his hand and a motorbike helmet under his arm. I released Brigitte so she could say something witty or flirty, and make him, finally, notice her.

"Bye, Scott," she said. Not exactly glittering repartee, but at least it was something.

"Yeah, yeah, um, see ya ..."

Brigitte, I wanted to shout. Her name is *Brigitte*. My name is Lucy and we've just spent the past four hours working together in a tiny tiled room covered with gravy stains. Remember? He didn't.

"I wish your dad would hurry up," I said, crossing my arms over my inadequate chest and stamping my feet to stay awake. I could just make out Mrs Hargraves in the shadows between the cars. She had dropped her car keys and was searching for them, giggling and carrying on. When I thought about her sleazy husband, I felt sorry for her.

"Here, let me," Scott scooped up her keys and put them in the ignition for her. She leaned up against him, whispered something and then laughed throatily.

"Sorry. Gotta go, Mrs H," he said, thumping her car roof. He put on his helmet and kick-started his Triumph, once, twice. It jumped forward a little, the thin tyres spitting out gravel.

"He's *so* hot," breathed Brigitte. We watched him roar off and I wondered if he was heading over to the oval where all the cool kids would be, hanging out and breaking the rules and a heap of hearts. I sniffed at my sleeve. I smelled of sausage rolls and sour spilled wine.

"Do you think he'll be working next weekend?" Brigitte said. "Oh, look. Here's Dad," she flagged him down. "Hey, Dad, don't forget we're taking Lucy home."

"I would never forget such an important mission as that," Mr Riley said sincerely. That's because Brigitte's dad was probably the nicest dad ever, apart from mine. Last holidays, he drove us up to Hornsby for Cold Rock Ice Cream to celebrate my coming home and getting the scholarship.

"Hi, Mr Riley," I said, climbing into the car and settling in the back next to Winston, Brigitte's geriatric corgi who liked to drool on my sneakers. He sniffed me and wagged his tail weakly at my eau de sausage-roll aroma. I patted his head and pulled over the rug that Mr Riley had brought, along with a thermos of hot chocolate, knowing that we had probably been too busy to eat.

"I know what a tyrant your boss is," he winked because the club's social secretary was his sister as well as Brigitte's aunt.

Twenty minutes later we were home.

"Don't forget you're coming over next weekend," Brigitte called out of the back window as Mr Riley swung the car out of my driveway.

When I got into bed, I lay there waiting for sleep, my feet aching, and my thoughts blurring as if I was on a carousel. First, I was at the bus stop with Natasha and two boys with dusty feet were chatting us up. Then, as if by magic, I was at the oval. I imagined myself there sitting cross-legged on top of the toilet block, feeling the warmth of the day radiating out from the concrete. I was hanging out with my cool-as-can-be friends. I had a boyfriend and I was wearing his hoodie. Every now and again he would lean across and kiss me and all my friends would go "ahhhhhh" because it was so romantic.

Chapter 3

My Sunday morning habit has always been to put on my over-sized periodic-table T-shirt, sharpen my pencils and get down to work. When I woke up, I couldn't give a damn about homework or anything. Perhaps I was coming down with something: Ebola or Swine flu or, maybe, that Zika virus. I felt my glands. Were they swollen? I couldn't find them. Was that a good sign or a bad one?

"How's the study?"

Mum had come into my room with an arm-full of clean washing, trailed by my two mini-dachshunds.

"Fine."

I watched her open and close drawers like she was part of a Netflix show. I was like a zombie. I didn't even move when my phone buzzed. A text.

"Aren't you going to look at that?"

Mum looked over-the-top horrified. I rolled my eyes.

"Ha, ha, very funny."

Mum eventually took the hint and left the room.

It was Natasha.

What's up? Lots of smiley faces.

I wonder what she wants? I shut my bedroom door and with slippery fingers called her.

"I'm not taking calls right now, but leave me a message. I'll call you. Promise." Her voice was low and husky and deliberately seductive, like she had a steady stream of callers she had to manage.

"Um, it's me, Lucy returning your call, um text," my voice went up like a squeaky question mark at the end, but I pushed on, "I'm home tonight, but if I go out, you know, I'll have my phone so you can call me. Anytime. I don't go to bed. I mean, I do, but not until really late. Anyway, I'll send you a text. Just in case you don't get this message."

She didn't call or text me back. So, Monday morning, early, I searched the locker room, the playground and finally, the library for her.

Just as I was giving up I found her sitting near the science lab, going through her make-up purse. Two backpacks were on the ground, but the owners were nowhere in sight. For some reason that made me nervous.

"Hi," I said, too loudly and sitting down so quickly my skirt made a balloon.

"Oh, hi." Natasha didn't look up. "Aha." She pulled out a mascara wand. "Found you. Hold this, would you." She handed me a little mirror and, bending closer, began to coat her lashes.

"I didn't think we could wear make-up to school," I said watching her.

"Mascara isn't make-up," she replied, her eyes half open, her mouth, too, in concentration.

"There. How do I look?" blinking rapidly at me.

"Brilliant," I said.

"You are funny," said Natasha. But I could tell she was pleased. I could see two of her deputies – Lindsay and Emma, I think – returning; I had to be quick.

"What did you want to talk to me about?"

"Huh?" Natasha was still examining herself from all angles.

"You rang me."

"I texted."

"Oh, yeah, right. But I called you back."

"I hope you don't take this the wrong way, but can I just tell you something. You should have returned my text with a text. Don't worry about it, though, it's a little thing."

She zippered up her purse and tucked it into her school bag.

"Oh, okay. What did you want?"

"Doesn't matter now."

"Oh, okay."

I rallied. "Oh, well, ring me when you remember. Or text me. Whatever," I added quickly when I caught the look on her face.

Then she said: "Have you done your English question? Is *Lady Macbeth* evil blah blah?"

I nodded.

"Cool. Can I borrow it?" She glanced at her nail beds, "I'm a bit stuck."

I made a mental note to practise the same nonchalant gesture later in the bathroom mirror.

"Sure," I said and stooped, knees popping, to open my bag. I handed her the sheet of paper that took me about a billion hours to write.

"Thanks. I owe you." She showed me her perfect white teeth and we walked into class together.

Natasha perched on a chair, knees sideways, up the back. There was a vacant seat beside her and room to get past her if I dared.

"I think your, ah, *friend* is trying to catch your attention," she murmured, and the way she said 'friend' left me in no doubt of her thoughts on that. I looked across to Brigitte who had saved me a seat up the front. With a pantomime of waves and eye movements I informed her I wouldn't be sitting with her today, that I'd catch her after class. Then I slowly moved into the spare seat beside Natasha. She showed me her folder cover. It was orange and in Comic Sans typeface was written the poem: 'God, grant me the serenity to accept the things I cannot change, courage to change the things I can, and wisdom to know the difference.'

"It's my mum's anthem," she whispered. "Not bad if you're, like, a loser."

I hid my own, covered in boring brown paper and plastic contact, underneath my banana pencil case which had looked hilariously ironic in IGA but now just looked lame.

"Where did you get your dolphin necklace?" said Natasha. We stood as the teacher walked in, me running my finger over the outline of the cord beneath my tunic. Under the cover of an exercise book into which we were supposed to be writing the comedic devices in *Taming of the Shrew*, I whispered from the corner of my mouth: "My great aunt gave it to me for my birthday."

"Can I have it?"

I stood completely still, a rabbit in headlights. The pendant was a precious possession; so delicate, such fine silver. There were even two tiny glass chips for its eyes. I adored it. I couldn't just give it away. Or could I? Natasha had already been pretty generous with me, giving me a lift and that fragrance. We were friends. Before I could change my mind, I unfastened it from around my neck and held it out. She took it and, looking straight ahead, casually dropped it into her blazer pocket.

After class as we left the classroom together and proceeded along the hallway to the usually dim, dusty science block, I was nearly blinded by a light, the kind found streaming through the domed Gothic windows of cathedrals on postcards. Standing next to Natasha Fielding it was as if I was suffused with the same light.

Like all good things, it would come at a price, but it was one that I was willing to pay. As I saw it, I had nothing to lose. All I had to do was to stay close to this vision and allow her popularity to rub off onto me. I would no longer be small and intense with a savings plan. No more boring me. I would be exciting, fun, dangerous. I would go to wild parties and have *experiences*. I would break hearts. Most of all, I wouldn't be invisible or forgettable or mousy.

And in science on that Monday afternoon, instead of writing down the method to an experiment, I made a list: hair, white ankle socks, double ear piercings, fake tan, boyfriend, new friends. I took out my low and neat regulation ponytail and retied it high and messy and stared at my list. With a new hairstyle and Natasha by my side, life would be different, shinier, better. I was as sure of that as I had been about anything in my life before. I didn't give a thought to the friendship I was about to destroy or the cost of not being true to myself. I was 15 and fickle. But that was no excuse at all.

Chapter 4

Tuesday morning, I had my face in *The Fault in Our Stars*, my go-to nostalgia read, and kept walking into people.

"Hey!"

"Look where you're going."

"Sorry."

"Sorry."

I was at the best bit – the part where Hazel and Gus travel to Amsterdam to meet her favourite author. I used to want to meet Enid Blyton – bit hard as she was dead but I was into time travel back then. I wondered who it would be now. John Green? Mark Haddon? Veronica Roth? At least they were all alive …

Bam.

"Watch it."

"Sorry. Oh, hey, it's you." Still half-transfixed by the world of cancer kids, I blinked myopically at Natasha, Emma and Lindsay.

"Hey," said Natasha. "I've been looking for you."

"Have you?" I turned down the edge of my page and closed the book on it. "Hi, everyone," I said. "Um, have you seen the movie? I'm up to the bit where they fly to Amsterdam."

Natasha nodded, "Yeah, yeah. Nothing beats a dying man's love." I looked at her closely. Was she being sarcastic? Weird. Everyone loved that book.

"We've got geography next, right?" I said.

After a pause, Lindsay nodded. When would she stop viewing me as the enemy?

"Not me," Natasha said.

"I do," said Emma. I looked from Lindsay to Emma. Noticed their closed-off expressions. When would they realise that I just wanted to be friends?

"I've gotta run." Natasha turned away. Then turned back, "What are you doing Friday afternoon?"

"Nothing. Why?"

"You can come over if you like."

"Really? I'd love to," I said.

"Great," said Natasha. She gave me a finger wave and left Lindsay and Emma and me in an awkward triangle.

"Linds, will you come with me to my locker before class?"

"Sure." As they headed towards the stairs, I heard Lindsay say, "Why did Natasha invite *her*?"

I couldn't hear Emma's answer.

***

Friday morning, I met Brigitte on the corner of Trafalgar Street, as usual, so we could walk to school together. Straightaway she could tell that I was in a tizz.

"What's wrong with you?" was the first thing she said.

"Why do you think something's wrong?"

"I don't know. Maybe because you're wearing odd socks and muttering to yourself." She scrutinised me.

"Oh that." I glanced down and saw that I was indeed wearing a blue sock and one white one. "I'm fine. I've got a test and I haven't studied." I said the first thing that came to me.

"Now I definitely know something's wrong. You've never not studied in your life." Brigitte looked worried. She kicked a gum nut out of the way. "Come over this afternoon. We can go to the pool and you can time me while I do my laps. I have the State championships coming up."

"Oh, Briggy, I can't. I'm going over to Natasha's this afternoon."

Brigitte's step faltered.

"What? You've been at the school for less than a term and you're already hanging out with the cool people. I've been there for nearly four years and I don't think Natasha and her gang have ever spoken to me." She was bewildered more than upset.

I gave her arm a squeeze. "That's not fair. Next time I'll get you an invite." I said it without thinking. If I had been, I'd never have promised what wasn't mine to give. Anyhow, there would probably not be a next time. I was so nervous, I was bound to stuff up and Natasha would never invite me over again.

I was a salmon twitching upstream at home time as I faced the girls teeming out the front gate in search of Natasha. I spied her and waved. She raised her left eyebrow and unhurriedly made her way towards me, her entourage trailing behind. My heart fluttered for a moment at their scowls.

"Hi." Natasha appeared unaware of any tension. I forced myself to relax. "Hi," I answered, and swung into step with them.

We walked up the street two by two. Lindsay and Natasha first, then Emma and I. Lindsay Penn, an almost pretty blonde with slightly protruding eyes, was Natasha's best friend. Emma Jenkins was number two. She had no bust to speak of and hid the fact behind a padded bra. She didn't speak one word to me as we trudged up to the station, cross that she was stuck with me. I tried anyway.

I noticed that she'd replaced the three regulation blue buttons at the neck of our summer tunic with three pale love hearts, each one attached with fluoro green thread.

"I like those buttons. Did you do them?" I said. She didn't answer.

I tried again. "Are we allowed to do that? Change things on our uniform?"

"Absolutely. You should definitely do something different to yours," said Emma, smiling almost to herself.

She said no more, listening in on Lindsay and Natasha in front, who were discussing last weekend's party at the oval and what a fool Kim had made of herself over some guy on a pushie. Apparently, he'd committed the sin of strapping a small engine to it to make it sound like a motorbike when he pedalled and ended up the laughing stock of the oval crowd.

"What a loser!" Emma leaned forward and spoke with relish.

"Kim was impressed. You should have seen her. She was all over him. It made me sick," said Lindsay. She passed a segment of mandarin to Natasha, and one to Emma, who moved up beside them.

"Thanks, Linds," said Emma, sucking on her segment.

Lindsay didn't offer one to me.

We spent ages in the newsagent's opposite the crossing, flicking through magazines.

"Would you look at her? Emma held up a picture of a goddess in a red bikini, kneeling on a pristine beach. "She's perfect."

"Wish I could look like that," Lindsay said. "I'm going on a diet."

"You know who that is?" said Natasha, snatching the magazine and peering. "Elle. Her sister's a year above at our school. She's modelling as well."

"You could be a model, Natasha," said Lindsay.

I was across the aisle, quietly testing silver and purple pens on the back of my hand.

"Nah, I couldn't," said Natasha, smoothing down her hair. "Could I?"

We missed the train. It was pulling away as we reached the stairs and the acrid smell of metal tickled my nose. We had a 15-minute wait for the next one and, as we crossed our legs and lowered ourselves onto the concrete platform, I realised that was the point. We sat in a circle, Natasha and Lindsay facing out and Emma and I with our backs to the tracks and the rose gardens opposite platform two. My uniform made a cottony hammock between my knees and I had to push it down so as not to flash the Grammar boys who had begun to thunder onto the platform.

"Anyone worth talking to?" said Natasha. She hadn't worried about her uniform flying up and was busy pulling something from the front of it.

It was the magazine she'd been examining at the newsagent.

"Nah. The train's here anyway," said Lindsay.

There was a whoosh of air over my head as a train slid into the station. We slowly stood. The slipstream pushed my fringe out of my eyes and a tall boy moved into my vision. His bag was over one shoulder and his black hair was falling into his eyes. He was a god.

"Who's that?" I hissed to Natasha. She glanced over to where I was ogling my eyes.

"Nick Hall?" she squeezed my hand in sympathy. "He's pretty cute, but he's got a girlfriend. Wait." She jerked my hand. "He's looking this way. Whoah, he's checking you out."

"Is he? Oh, God." I looked sideways and pulled down my skirt.

"No, don't look." Natasha held me firmly. A gust of wind from the approaching train blew hot air into my face. It was more likely he was checking out Natasha. I hitched my bag up and my dress down, stepped into the train and sneaked a second peek just as the doors were closing. My bag became caught in the rubber lips of the doors. I yanked it and stumbled into Emma.

"Lucy!" She made my name sound long and annoying.

"Sorry." I hung onto her arm for a second, then straightened and stared out the window. I didn't feel

Emma's sting or see the brown and red ribbon of houses whizzing by. All I noticed was a Grammar boy with dark eyes.

* * *

The blowflies in my stomach had returned by the time we reached Natasha's house. It was one of two massive concrete bunkers, both two-storey with double garages. I could see the foliage of a giant oak tree in the backyard of the house further along, that every autumn must have clogged the pool filter with its rust-coloured leaves. Was that Natasha's house? It wasn't. Hers had a square-stepped water feature in the front and a portico where the girls were milling around and throwing their bags. Natasha used the spare key from under a mat the size of a playing field to open her oversized front door.

We followed her through the house, Natasha turning on every light even though it was only 3.30 in the afternoon. Mr Fielding wasn't at home, of course; nor was Simone, Natasha's older sister. Mrs Fielding, I found out, didn't live there.

"Where is she?" I asked Lindsay, fixing her hair at the bathroom mirror.

"This really great place in Manly," she paused, mid-fluff, then decided there was no harm in telling me everything. "She dumped Natasha's father when

Natasha was 8 and her sister was 13." Apparently, living in an ashram with her guru was better than being a mother of two daughters. It turned out communal living didn't suit her.

We took our Coke Zeros and a packet of Tim Tams into Natasha's bedroom and flopped down on our stomachs making a circle in the middle of the shredded grey carpet that reeked of talcum powder and dust.

I thought I was there to help them with their homework, but Natasha had other ideas, ordering shoes off so that Lindsay could paint everyone's toenails.

She started with Natasha, and with careful strokes, painted them a lurid purple frost, snapping a picture of her handiwork when she was done.

"Who's next?" she said.

"Me!" shouted Emma so I began to examine Natasha's bedroom. There was a queen-sized bed, pushed to the wall. On it was a white satin bedspread, but rumpled and tangled with clothes. There was a door – leading to the walk-in wardrobe, I guessed, and probably filled with Tiger Lily and Zara, stores stocking the kinds of expensive clothes my mother deplored – and a white narrow chest of long drawers slung with beads and loaded up with an assortment of fragrance bottles and make-up.

"What about Lucy next," said Natasha. I glanced up. Lindsay looked hard at Natasha but obediently reached for my feet. While they dried, we flicked through Natasha's Instagram to look at the pictures posted by girls in our class.

Lindsay talked first: "Cute shot. Fiona is pretty enough to be a seven but what she did last week to Daniel, dumping him on Facebook, was way harsh. She only deserves a five."

"I love what Laura's done with her hair. Her fringe is totally there and she's got a thigh gap. She's definitely an eight now. She's nearly ready to hang out with us," Emma drew her breath. "But only if she dumps that loser with the braces." The others agreed.

They went on like that for ages. I switched off and went back to checking out Natasha's bedroom. It was as luxurious as I'd expected but a lot messier.

"What do you think, Lucy?"

"Umm, I totally agree about the thigh gap and braces thing. Love it."

"What? The braces or the thigh gap?"

"Err, both. I love what she's done with the wristbands," I rambled on. "Multicoloured, so like Gay Pride and everything."

Lindsay and Emma exchanged looks.

It went on and on until dusk and Emma and Lindsay both said they had to go; they had to be home by 5.30 or else.

Mum couldn't pick me up until 6.30, after Milly's ballet lesson, so I stayed for dinner. We sat up at the island bench while Mr Fielding, who'd come home while we were painting our nails and put on dinner, pulled the roast chicken and potatoes out of the oven.

"Hey, Natasha, you're not really a princess so lay the table," Mr Fielding ordered. She rolled her eyes but got up and rummaged around in the cutlery drawer coming back with what we needed.

"Where's Simone? Is she coming home for dinner?"

"Your sister is working until 8. Doormat Dave is picking her up and they're seeing a movie or something. Don't forget napkins."

"You can't be bothered with food half the time. And yet we have to have linen napkins," complained Natasha. "Can't you see the hypocrisy in that, Dad?" But she retrieved them from the hutch in the hall just the same.

I ate up. I loved roast chicken. Mr Fielding didn't say anything to start with except for, "Pass the pepper". Natasha and I talked about school and her sister's new boyfriend, who was called Doormat Dave because "he does everything she says. It's pathetic."

"Leave your sister alone," said Mr Fielding. "And concentrate on your own problems like getting better marks in your exams. Or you'll be at the local school so fast it will make your head swim."

Natasha barely swallowed a bite of her dinner. I didn't notice at first, but when I stood to help stack the plates, I saw that she'd shredded the chicken and scattered it about her plate and pushed the peas under her fork. Mr Fielding hadn't noticed, he'd moved down to the other end of the bench to where the phone and bills were and sat there on and off the phone yakking about payment plans. Natasha and I scraped and rinsed the plates and set them in the dishwasher.

"Did your dad mean that? About the state school?" I said as we put the knives and forks upside down in the basket and arranged the pans so the door could close. They were regular chores, the sort I did at home every night of the week. Funny, I hadn't thought of Natasha doing anything so mundane.

"Nah, he's full of it," she said, but her eyes were shards of glass.

As I hung the tea towel over the oven door, like I did at home, the doorbell went and I heard my mum introduce herself to Mr Fielding.

"Thanks for having me," I said to Mr Fielding as I passed him in the hallway.

"No problem. Thanks for tutoring Natasha," he said. What did he mean by tutoring? Before I could ask, he'd moved on to, of all things, tennis. Did I play?

Should I lie or tell the truth? Mum fixed me with one of her death stares. I gulped, hoping it wouldn't cost me the invitation, "Erm, not very well."

"Doesn't matter, I've hired a court next Thursday. Come and have a hit with us and the new neighbours next door. Name of Curtis and they've got two boys about your age."

Chapter 5

On Saturday afternoon, my mother dropped me over to the Riley house on her way to take Milly to ballet.

Brigitte met me not at the front door but at the side door used only by family and family friends like me.

"I haven't seen you for ages," she said letting me in. "Want a drink?" I nodded and walked without blinking down her hall, past her bedroom and her bed that was covered with about a gazillion stuffed animals – Brigitte was a keen collector of cute things – and into the kitchen where Brigitte pulled a two-litre plastic bottle of cordial from the fridge. Oh, bliss. It was a water-or-milk-only zone at my place. I was onto my second cup when her brother sidled into the room.

"Hi, Dork," I said. It was supposed to be our little joke, but he looked crestfallen. "Hey, what's up?"

"Nothing," he said, taking a clean cup from the dishwasher and thumping it down on the bench, his way of asking me to fill it up. Which I did.

"How're Sid and Nancy? I've got a business going: dog-walking. I'll walk them for you, if you want. Five dollars a dog."

"Highway robbery, Noah. They only have little legs. They need half the walk. What's your best offer?"

Noah thought for a bit. "Five dollars for both."

"How far will you walk them?"

"Three times around the oval," said Noah, quickly.

"Okay. I'll check with my mum and get back to you."

Noah nodded again. He couldn't expect fairer than that.

"How's Nev?" Neville was Noah's mangy cockatoo. He always looked so tragic that I expected to hear at any moment that he'd dropped off the perch.

"Great. I've taught him a new word."

"What is it?" I asked. "Help?"

"I'll show you." He grabbed my hand and pulled me outside to where Nev's rundown cage sat on top of an old chest of drawers on the wooden deck.

"Isn't he awesome?" said Noah, enraptured. "Smart, too."

"Umm." I eyeballed Brigitte extravagantly.

"You can pat him. Just this once," he said, generously.

"Wow, Noah, I'm lucky." I reached in to the cage. Nev, however, disagreed. He darted forward and gave me a nip.

I nursed my injured finger in the palm of my other hand.

"Cut that out, Nev. Sorry, Lucy. Well, do you want to hear the word?"

I nodded, and put my throbbing finger in my mouth in an effort to cool it down.

Nev glared at us, silent.

"He's a bit shy today," said Noah, putting his hand in the cage to pat his beloved pet and crooning. Nev looked smug.

"Shy?" Brigitte gave a derisive snort. "We'll have to give you a rabies shot, Lucy." She saw Noah's face and quickly said, "Just kidding. I'll get you a Band-Aid."

"You've got a misogynistic cockatoo in there," I mumbled, still sucking my finger.

"Jump in the lake!" Nev shrieked. Noah beamed.

"Good one, Nev. He's never said so many words in one go. That's called a conversation, Nev."

I took my finger out of my mouth long enough to mumble: "Nice."

Brigitte's little brother was unusual, but I liked him. He kept insects, and not always in Bug Catchers.

He had a cardboard box full of silkworm eggs under his bed and a cage lined with newspapers for his pet mice in the carport. He sold these to kids at his school for $1 each and bought back for 50 cents a week later when mothers insisted the mice had to go. His conversations always began with, "Did you know?" That got tedious, except this one time when he told my mum that platypuses could only copulate in running water. She was politely amazed, much to Noah's gratification. Mostly he left us alone. He didn't barge into Brigitte's bedroom if we had the door closed like some other people I knew.

"How's school?" I said.

"All right, I suppose," he said. "But I don't like my new maths teacher. He's mean and when he talks, he spits on everyone in the front row, sometimes even the second. I get to class late every Wednesday because I have a violin lesson at recess and only the front row seats are left. I've told Mum to change my music lesson but she won't."

Noah gloomily put Nev back on his perch. Nev puffed up angrily.

"Kiss me. Kiss me, Kiss me." So Noah did.

"Yuck," I said. I meant the kiss, but Noah said, "I know. I need an umbrella in class."

Brigitte returned with a Band-Aid.

"Noah's been put into a special class for geniuses," she said handing it to me.

"Thanks." I wound it round my finger.

"You could give him some tips about that," she said.

"No. I couldn't." I glared at her.

"Don't be cross, Lucy. I just meant that you're really clever, too."

"Sorry, but I'm sick of being the weird brainy girl."

I crumpled up the Band-Aid wrapping. "What do you want to do?"

"Let's rollerblade up and down Dr Griffin's driveway. They've gone out. I'll teach you the double drop." I was about to protest that rollerblading was for babies when I saw Brigitte's hopeful face.

"Let's," I said.

Brigitte took off first, her arms outstretched, gathering speed as she bumped over the uneven surface. She took the turn with a whoop and clattered to a stop near the garage door.

"Your turn."

"Yay," I said, weakly. My sense of balance was notoriously bad.

"You can do this." She held my outstretched arm and walked with me most of the way.

"Ready?"

"No," I gasped, but she gave me a push anyway. "Go, go, go!"

I fell over, skidding along the uneven surface like a bowling ball going into the gutter. Brigitte helped me up and set me down on the grass verge between the cars.

"Are you all right? Does it hurt?" she asked. We both peered at the beads of blood escaping my grazed knees.

"Not much. They're kinda hot, though," I said, and blew on them. "I won't be able to do any pole dancing for a while."

Brigitte didn't laugh.

"What? It was a joke." I fanned my knees. Brigitte fell down by my side.

"Sorry. I guess I've got other things on my mind."

I looked across at her.

"It's nothing, really." She leaned forward so that her hair partly covered her face, which always meant *something*. "It's just that Scott's been fired."

"How come?"

"He was caught with Deborah in the storeroom," she paused, "Lucky Deborah."

Personally, I didn't think so. "How did you find out?"

"My aunt told me."

"Maybe the new guy will be even cuter," I said.

"Yeah, maybe." Brigitte gave me a lopsided smile. "So, what did you do the other day at Natasha's?"

"Nothing much," I said, stretching out on the verge. "We painted our nails and did homework."

"What's Natasha's house like?"

"I thought she'd live in a palace, you know, but it was sort of normal like yours." I chewed my lip. "Nicer than mine, though."

"But you're only renting 'til your dad gets a full-time job." Brigitte loyally patted my hand. "Tell me more about Natasha."

"Well, her parents are divorced."

"That figures," Brigitte said meaningfully.

"What does that mean?"

"Well, you know …"

"Not really." I didn't want to hear anything negative about Natasha.

"Sorry." Brigitte subsided into silence. Eventually, she spoke.

"What's going on with you?"

"What do you mean?" But I had an idea she was talking about my fascination with Natasha. I couldn't explain it to myself let alone to Brigitte. I sat up and began to undo the rollerblades.

"You've been all weird lately." Brigitte's voice wobbled. "Have I done something to annoy you?"

"No!" I pulled my rollerblades off and they clattered into the gutter.

"It's nothing." I put the boots together. "I've just been a bit stressed. New school, you know, it's like …" I made a gesture with my hands around my ears to illustrate my head exploding.

"Oh, okay," Brigitte said slowly. "I get it. You're doing really well, though. All the girls really like you. You're even getting noticed by the popular group. But I should warn you," Brigitte leaned forward. "Natasha is two-faced."

But I wasn't really listening by then. My phone had begun to vibrate. I had a text. I scooped it up. It was from Natasha.

What are you doing?

Nothing much.

Come over

I can't

We're going to the oval ...

What time?

Meeting at 8. Everyone's going.

Who was everyone? Nick Hall? I bit my lip. What should I reply? I longed to type YES. But I was staying, like always, at Brigitte's until Mum picked me up at 9. I couldn't just leave. Or could I? What if I said I was feeling sick and went home early? But then I'd have to explain to Mum why, if I was so sick, I was planning to hang out at the oval. I glanced over at Brigitte who had become tired of waiting and got up to practise her turns, her arms flailing and her mouth open in concentration. I couldn't do it. My shoulders slumped as I sent back my answer. When Brigitte's mum brought out a plate of muesli slice squares, I ate three, one after the other, until I felt sick for real.

Later on, after the magpies had started up their evening call, Mrs Riley put pizza on the table. Then Brigitte and I watched *Doctor Who* on ABC iView with Noah while Mrs Riley ironed Mr Riley's shirts and Mr Riley napped in the Jason Recliner with a newspaper resting on his belly.

"Did you have fun?" Mum asked on the way home.

"Okay, I suppose," I said. "Can I ask you something? Do you like ironing Dad's shirts?"

"*Like* is a bit of a stretch," Mum said. "I do it because I love him. And because it costs $3 a shirt if I send them to Rita."

"When I grow up, I'm not going to iron my husband's shirts," I said. "I don't care how much I love him."

Chapter 6

On Thursday, the day we met the Curtis boys, it was 30 degrees, and all the gardenia flowers in the garden were turning yellow and dying.

Natasha had arranged for us to do homework in her room beforehand, sprawled and hot in front of open books and a packet of lamington fingers. This time, I didn't feel quite so out of place and when I leaned over to change one of her answers it seemed like the most natural thing in the world. At two minutes to five, Mr Fielding banged on the door, and told us to get a wriggle on or else.

Natasha jumped up and peeled off her uniform to reveal Lycra shorts underneath and a purple bra with satin trim. She shrugged on a white singlet, the purple bra showing through. I had brought along a pair of denim cut-offs and a loose faded yellow T-shirt that, when I put it on, made me resemble a lemon.

When we arrived at the park, Mr Fielding leapt out of the car and began an elaborate stretching routine, touching his toes and swinging his racquet behind his shoulders to loosen up, while Natasha and I bashed an old hairy tennis ball to each other, and waited, breath held in the stillness of the afternoon.

Natasha saw them first. She threw the ball in the air and served. It went straight for my head. Or so it seemed. I ducked instinctively, collapsing backwards on my elbows and haunches in a most unladylike fashion. I heard a guffaw and I turned, and there they were: two tall brothers, both looking amused but also sort of appraising.

"Hello, lads," said Mr Fielding, still flexing his muscles. I didn't know if he was trying to frighten or impress them. He was pretty fit for an old guy.

"Where are your folks?"

"Hi, Sir, thanks for inviting us. My parents rang to say that they're stuck at work. They'll be here as soon as they can." Hugh shook his hand, firmly, which seemed to impress Mr Fielding judging by the enthusiastic way he kept pumping on Hugh's arm.

I looked more closely at him while he spoke. Hugh was definitely the older of the two. He was lean with quiet grey eyes that held on to Mr Fielding's gaze quite steadily. I wondered if Natasha's stomach was doing flip flops like mine. It was funny how my body reacted these days to any fit-looking guy.

Sam wasn't quite as handsome; his face was too angular, his nose too snub, for that, but it was an open and friendly face and I would have quite warmed to him had he not sniggered so rudely at my uncoordinated fall.

Still, he loosened up the atmosphere on the court no end, describing the game like a radio announcer. Even Hugh cracked a smile.

"Fielding and Johnson are down two games to four. Their freakishly good-looking opponents are about to comfortably win the set thanks to superb ball skills and a superior strategy."

I poked out my tongue and prepared to serve, bouncing the ball a couple of times before sending it high above my head. My racquet caught the ball on the wood and flung it wide. Sam stretched for it, caught it on the edge and the ball made it back over the net. He cheered himself in a most unsportsmanlike way.

After a while, Natasha, with a slip of a smile, peeled off her sloppy joe to reveal her figure beneath her singlet and Lycra shorts. I wished my legs looked like hers in Lycra. We kept playing, but the boys lost their concentration and we won 6:4. Natasha elbowed Sam as they forced their way through the gate at the same time. Sam fell back, his hand on his heart, and Natasha stalked across the patchy lawn to the bubbler next to the wooden picnic table, her hoodie draped over one shoulder and leaned over to drink. I became aware of a change of atmosphere. Everyone was relaxed, sure, but watchful, too, and careful not to show it.

"Will we play mixed doubles now?" Natasha had finished with drinking and was scooping palmfuls of water over her neck. Little trickles ran into the shadow between her breasts.

"Does your dad want to have a game?" said Hugh dutifully, looking in the direction of Mr Fielding. We looked, too. He was reading the paper in the car, seat reclined all the way, and the radio on.

"Doesn't look like it," said Sam.

"Who's going to play with me?" said Natasha.

"Me!"

"I will!"

Natasha laughed.

"Poor Lucy. She'll get a complex."

I spent a long time, red-faced, fiddling with my shoelace and feeling lousy in my knee-length shorts and T-shirt. I should have been wearing Lycra and flirting. *BuzzFeed* always stressed the importance of playful sexiness in the seduction game. What was the flirting checklist? Toss hair; hold stare; touch forearm; show flesh. Frankly, that all seemed too obvious and silly. How could you possibly do it with a straight face? Surely the guys on the receiving end didn't fall for it? Apparently, they did. Sam and Hugh were pathetic the way they were fighting for Natasha's attention. What was wrong with just being yourself? And what was so good about being treated like an object anyhow?

"Get your big fat bums back on the court, girls," said Mr Fielding. He had finished with the paper and was strolling towards us, flashing his racquet left and right like a sword. "Who's for a dustup?"

For an instant, Natasha seemed … Annoyed? Petulant? Then her expression blanked and her shoulders went up in a shrug. Hugh put up his hand and said. "I'll take you on."

Natasha sat on the grass, her chin on her knees, her eyes following the play. I was sprawled beside her, feeling the prickle of the buffalo grass on my bare legs and trying to come up with something clever to say to Hugh when he came off the court or something funny for Sam, who was dozing beside me. Instead, all I ended up with was a bracelet I'd woven out of clover flowers that attracted bees when I slipped it over my wrist and a headache from trying too hard.

Still, tennis must have been deemed a success because arrangements were made for a rematch the following week.

Suddenly, Natasha and I were united in a common interest: the Curtis boys. Not that we ever said so, but the following day – Friday – I found her at my locker just before the morning bell and we walked together to class.

"Thanks again for inviting me to play tennis last night," I said. "And for dropping me home afterwards."

"Hey, meet me at my locker after school, and we'll go to the station together."

I felt the warmth of acceptance creep up my neck and then down to my stomach. "Okay."

When I arrived at her locker, Lindsay and Emma were already circling. But, really, what did I expect? That she was mine exclusively? Again, I walked with Emma behind Natasha and Lindsay, Emma's mouth puckering up when she saw that she was stuck with me again.

I felt like saying, "Ditto, sister," but wisely held my tongue.

We hit the station at the same time as the Grammar boys. I spotted Sam in the throng, and lifted my arm to wave.

"Stop that," hissed Natasha. "You look desperate." Emma and Lindsay swivelled in interest. "Do you know him?"

"Um." I glanced to Natasha for guidance. She shook her head slightly.

"Not really."

"Don't look now. But there's Nick Hall. He's so gorgeous." Lindsay spoke huskily out of the side of her mouth. "Who's that he's next to? I haven't seen him before. He's cute, too."

We all sneaked a look. It was Hugh Curtis and he was standing next to Nick Hall, the tall dark-haired guy who'd bottomed out my stomach last week. And, wouldn't you know, he did it again. He's got a girlfriend, I reminded myself.

Natasha had made it clear that knowing the Curtis boys was to be our secret, at least for now. I didn't mind as it bound us together, the way secrets did. Sure enough, as I got out of the train, Natasha leaned forward, out of earshot of the others, and asked me over to stay the night on Saturday night.

Exactly 25 hours later, I sat in Natasha's room waiting for her older sister Simone to finish in the bathroom and leave. She was going on a date with a new guy, having ditched Doormat Dave, and she was late. I could hear her swearing and flinging her make-up into drawers. Slam, bang and, finally, she was gone, leaving soggy towels and balled up tissues in her wake. The house settled back to its original shape.

"What do you want to do? Homework?" I asked.

"God, no," Natasha looked me over like I was nuts. "Let's put a treatment in our hair."

I said, "What sort of treatment?"

"Just follow me."

In the bathroom, three pairs of Simone's navy work tights were dangling over the bath and Natasha tore them off to run the bath water.

"We have to dampen our hair. Here, you go first." She pushed my head under the tap.

"Oww. That's cold." I jerked my head out of reach.

"Don't be a baby." First my hand, and then, gingerly my head went back under the tap. When my hair was sufficiently wet, Natasha threw me one of Simone's musty, used towels. It smacked me in the face.

"Hey," I said and glared at her.

"Sorry," she said, not sounding a bit sorry. "This is for your own good. Your hair is really going to benefit from this."

With her own hair wrapped turban style, Natasha fished around in the bottom drawer for two of Simone's oil capsules. She handed me one and said, "Twist the top and then when I'm ready pour it over my head." She did the same to me and afterwards, while we waited for the oil to work through, I asked what Lindsay and Emma were doing tonight.

"I have no idea. Honestly, I'm a bit sick of those two at the moment. They really get on my nerves." Natasha dabbed her forehead with the edge of a towel and peered at herself in the mirror. "Hey, what's with your friend?"

"What? Who?" My heart already sinking at the look on Natasha's face. "You mean Brigitte?"

"Not that there's anything wrong with it or anything. But, is she, like, a lesbian?"

"No. Why do you say that?"

"Nothing. It's just that I've seen her checking me out." Natasha drew a comb through the front of her hair and held it down with her fingers. "Hey, do you think I should get a fringe?"

"Umm, maybe," I said cautiously, not quite sure if she'd finished with Brigitte. But she had. She continued to examine herself in the mirror. "I don't know …"

"Yes, definitely," I nodded firmly.

She kept her eyes on herself, "It would look amazing, wouldn't it?"

"Amazing," I repeated.

"When it's wet, your hair looks amazing too," Natasha returned the favour graciously.

"Really?" I had never thought of my hair as a particular feature, like, say, my eyes or my waist. It was somehow always too dark, too unruly, too much. It was not fair and sleek and obedient like Natasha's. It was my turn to regard myself in the mirror, "Thanks."

"You're welcome." Natasha turned on the hair dryer. "Check this out. I learned this trick on YouTube."

After we'd blow-dried our hair into oblivion and put on a homemade oatmeal mask using a recipe from the same YouTube series which dried tight on our skin, we finally talked about the Curtis boys through barely moving mouths. I couldn't quite believe that they lived next door to Natasha; at this very moment only a few metres from us. How could Natasha bear having them so close? I wouldn't be able to eat, concentrate or sleep a wink. But then, except for some country cousins who I only saw once a decade, I hadn't had a great deal to do with boys. And that was the way I'd liked it. Until this year.

"Have you seen them around?"

"Nah. I've seen their dad put out the rubbish, though."

"Do you think we'll see them tonight?"

"Maybe. I don't know."

She turned on the tap and began dabbing at her mask with a washer, tossing it back onto the bathroom floor when she'd finished. She peered in the mirror at the effect on her pores, smearing porridge on the edge of the vanity and the taps. Satisfied, she padded back to the bedroom.

"I think we should. Otherwise, why did we just do our hair?"

She opened her wardrobe. "Let's get dressed up and go over and ask for a couple of eggs."

"Why do we need eggs?"

"For the cake we're going to bake." Natasha was exasperated that I wasn't catching on.

"Oh."

Natasha looked me up and down and decided my shorts and T-shirt weren't up to much.

"Here, you can borrow this." She threw her playsuit at me, the one she was wearing the day I met her. It was much too long in the crutch on me, but I didn't care. I was finally wearing a playsuit. She scanned the room looking for something. She found it. It was a ribbon that dangled from a hook inside her wardrobe. Attached to it was a picture of her mum. She unpinned the picture, letting it slide to the floor so that she could use the ribbon to tighten the playsuit around my waist. "There." She stood back with one eye closed to look at me.

The shoe-string straps didn't quite cover my bra straps and the ribbon had made the shorts too short. But I didn't care. We brushed our hair, carefully applied two coats of mascara and a dousing of Simone's new Gucci fragrance. For a second we stood in the centre of the room, staring at each other, and I noticed with pride that Natasha was wearing my pendant. We were ready for anything and anyone.

Chapter 7

Sam answered the door, eating a banana. He didn't seem at all surprised to see us.

"Hi, Sam. Could you ask your mum if we can borrow a couple of eggs?"

"Mum's not here. What do you want eggs for?"

"We're making a cake."

"I'll go see if we've got any." He disappeared, leaving us at the door. Natasha went up and down on balls of her feet, winked and nudged her shoulder into mine. I didn't smile back. This was too embarrassing. He returned with a box of a dozen eggs.

"Is this enough?"

"We only need two," said Natasha, taking the box anyway.

"Yeah, well bring the rest back when you've finished," said Sam.

"We'll bring over some of the cake, too."

"Okay." Sam stood in the doorway and watched us walk all the way up his driveway and down Natasha's.

"There's a short-cut, you know," he called out, "through the hedge."

Later, the hedge almost became our undoing, catching the edge of our lumpy packet mix cake and nearly removing it altogether from the plate. I caught it just in time. I was still licking Betty Crocker frosting from my fingertips as Natasha rang the doorbell for the second time, the cake once again tipping precariously.

"Oh, give it to me," she said just before the door swung open.

This time, it was Hugh who stood before us, in cricket whites. He stared at us like we were from planet Mars. Sam mustn't have told him about us borrowing eggs.

Undaunted, Natasha thrust the plate towards him and said in her most winning way, "Here, we baked a cake as a thank you for, you know, lending us some eggs."

He stood still, taking in the cake that teetered in her outstretched arms without a word. Eventually, he turned his body a little so we could get past.

We crossed the lounge room and kept going, walking through a dining room with a galley kitchen and into a smaller room. In one corner, a fake wood fireplace; in the other, a television set. It was on mute and I could see men in white standing around a cricket pitch.

"Are your parents home?" I said, taking in the messy kitchen, a cricket bat and a pair of spiked boots on the coffee table.

"Nope," said Hugh. Sam wandered in and pulled up when he saw us. "Hey. Again."

"We brought you that cake like we promised," said Natasha.

"Excellent," he said politely.

We stood there.

I thought, *we've made a mistake in coming. They don't want us here.* I felt foolish and ran my palms down my sides to dry them.

"Want something to drink?"

"No, thank you." I used my best voice.

"Yes, please," said Natasha.

"Which is it?" said Sam with his head on the side and a smile that I saw could, sort of, sneak up on a person.

Hugh muttered something about getting changed. I waited until I heard the snap of the fridge door and of cans being pulled and poured out. I grabbed Natasha's arm.

"Oh, my God. We've got to get out of here."

"Why? Aren't you having fun? I am."

"You've got to be kidding. This is like having our nails pulled out with pliers." I fell silent as Sam returned with cokes in mismatched glasses. When Hugh came back, he stank of aftershave just like my dad when it was 'two for one' night at the club in Western Australia.

We sank down on the cream velour modular sofa: Sam, me, Natasha and Hugh at the other end. It was almost dark and I saw our reflections in the bare glass sliding doors that ran from the floor almost to the ceiling. This place was way too modern for curtains. I could just make out Hugh's profile as he rested his head against the brick wall, at ease and sure of himself. Even his ears were attractive.

Sam was as mobile as Hugh was anchored. Since we'd arrived, he'd refilled our glasses twice, twiddled with the TV remote and cracked open the sliding door to let in some air. It brought with it the faint drone of a pool filter and the burps of frogs caught up inside it. Now he was in the kitchen shaking Cheezels into one of those laminated wooden bowls that every family in our suburb had. Did he have ADHD? I jumped up and joined him, threading a Cheezel onto each pinky finger. "Do you like living here?"

"Yup." Sam pushed shut the cupboard above his head – it clicked into place – and turned to me.

"The view's pretty good. The window faces onto the Fieldings' back verandah."

I couldn't work out what he meant.

"It's a popular sunbaking spot," he explained.

"Oh." I nibbled at the Cheezel on my finger until I thought of something else to say. "Does this represent the dairy food group?"

"Five a day gives you your complete daily calcium requirements," said Sam in his best advertising voice.

"Better have another, then."

"I'm sure we've got Ribena somewhere here, so you can get your vitamin C quota, too."

We laughed together, pleased with our little joke.

"What is the age difference between you and Hugh?"

"18 months, but I'm only a year behind him at school."

"How come?"

"Dunno. I went up a grade, I guess." Sam busied himself at the kitchen counter. I took another Cheezel.

"How long can you stay?" he said after a while.

"Tonight? I'm not sure. I'm staying at Natasha's so it's kind of up to her."

Sam called through the door way to Natasha. "Are you going to stay?"

"Why not?

"We could play Halo."

Natasha wrinkled her nose at his suggestion.

"Or we could watch a movie," Sam went on. "You can choose."

"Shouldn't we check with your dad?" I called out. I didn't want Mr Fielding to be mad at us and label me a bad influence.

Natasha thought that was an insane idea and said so as I slid back down beside her.

"Excellent. What do you want to watch?" Sam flicked through the channels, settled on *Alien vs Predator*. What happened to us being able to choose? He dimmed the lights and bounced down next to me, putting an experimental arm around the back of the sofa behind my head. I glared at him. He removed his arm.

After a while, Natasha began to fidget. Soon she stood up and pushed past my legs to get to the open sliding door.

"Isn't it hot tonight?" she fanned herself, arched her back, picked up a magazine, wandered back to the sofa, flopped down. "Aren't you hot, Lucy?"

My eyes were hooked on the screen. I was into movies. Black and white, musicals, schlock, I loved them all. "Not really. A bit, maybe."

"What's your pool like?" Natasha flicked through *TV Week*, threw it back on the coffee table.

"Haven't been in yet," said Hugh. "Half the fence is missing and Dad's only just got the pH right."

"What happened to the fence?" I asked.

"A cricket ball smashed one of the glass panels," answered Sam.

"Hey," like Natasha had just thought of it, "Let's go for a swim."

"But we haven't got our costumes," I said, ever practical.

"That's the point." Natasha pinched me warningly on the arm. Play along, it said.

"What? Like a skinny dip?" Sam looked around, interested.

"Why not? I'm game if you are." Her eyes wouldn't let go of him.

Sam glanced at Hugh, who gave a little why not shrug, and at me.

"Nah," said Sam. He could see that I was freaking.

"Party pooper," she said, crossing her arms in a staged sulk.

Hugh took in her pout, her legs that went all the way up her denim skirt and the cleavage she'd maximised with crossed arms.

"Let's do it."

"What if a neighbour sees us?" I gulped. "What if Natasha's dad sees us? What if your parents come home?"

"Our Olds aren't coming home. They're in Canberra for the weekend. But I wouldn't want Mr Fielding to see his precious daughter swimming naked in my pool." But Hugh's eyes darkened all the same.

"Don't worry about him. What's the bet he's asleep in front of the telly? Anyway, I'm not going to swim *naked*. I'll keep my underwear on." And, with that, Natasha was outside, pulling off her clothes, tossing them aside and squealing a little as she slid into the water in just her bra and underpants.

"Come in. It's not cold at all." Her shoulders glistened in the moonlight before she dived under and swam to the other side, smiling to herself when Hugh appeared silhouetted in the doorway, light from the TV flickering behind his head. He stared at her, at her long pale hair streaming out, his expression inscrutable, and then he began to remove his jeans and T-shirt. He joined her in the deep end and they began swimming around and laughing. He moved in close to her, his dark head beside her blonde one. She splashed him with her fingers in a playful gesture, but the look they exchanged was anything but that. I felt that funny feeling again in the base of my stomach as I stood on the edge, the pavers scratching my feet. I didn't want to undress in front of them. I didn't even want to go swimming. I just wanted to finish the movie and have a cup of chamomile tea.

Splash. Sam dive-bombed into the pool, whooping with the shock. He surfaced and said slyly, "Come in, Lucy. We won't look," as if he could read my mind.

I stepped away from them, further back into the velvety darkness and thought about whether I would or wouldn't. Eventually, I began to undress. I undid the ribbon, my fingers fumbling a little, first, folding the playsuit carefully before creeping to the edge of the shallow end, my hands fanned strategically in front of my underwear. While Natasha and the boys circled one another, I lowered myself down onto the step until I was sitting neck deep and covered by the water.

"Lucy, you did it!" called out Natasha, swimming across to me in a few strokes. We sat side by side on the step watching Sam and Hugh staging a diving competition until Natasha pulled herself out. She stood there in her lacy white underwear, now see-through in the moonlight. The boys pretended not to look.

"Can I have a towel?" she called and Hugh, up the other end of the pool, skidded to the cabana, returning with four navy and white striped towels. He threw one in my general direction and wrapped the other around Natasha's shoulders with a great show of tenderness. She looked at him as he did it, the drips on her face and hair like silver beads.

I was left to my own devices. I clambered out of the pool and reached for a towel. Dripping and shivering, but triumphant that I'd actually gone skinny dipping – well, almost – I was now thankful that it was all over. I began to dress, the cotton snagging uncomfortably on my wet body. By the time Mr Fielding came outside, a shadow stretching on the back step that at first startled us and then made us giggle through our chattering teeth, we were dressed, we handed back the towels and then, breathlessly, pushed our way through the hedge as if we did it every night of the week.

The next day I woke early. For a second I couldn't work out where I was. Oh, yeah. That's right. I was on a foam mattress on the floor of Natasha's room. I wriggled, my sheets making a swishing sound, and poked a nose cautiously out. Her room looked different in the morning. Silver beams of dusty light caught on the edge of the old oak dresser and made mountains out of the humps of clothes. A couple of discarded dirty black shoe heels, half hidden under the bed.

My gaze shifted to the head on the pillow above me. I could just make out the edge of a pillowcase and a few strands of blonde hair. I reached out and tugged, once, quickly. She didn't stir so I lay on my back, cosy in my bed and thought about last night. I'd never done anything like that before. I wriggled my toes, feeling daring and mature. I didn't want to get up. I wanted to stay and think on about what we did, but I needed to use the bathroom. Damn. I struggled out of my bed and, after washing my hands, crept into the kitchen, pulling down on my T-shirt to partly hide my patchwork pyjama bottoms.

Mr Fielding was inserting a pod into his coffee machine, and its burnt smell turned my stomach a little. "Want a cup?" he said, not turning, and poured me one without waiting for a reply.

I sat down, took a sip and pulled a face. I hadn't tasted coffee before, just iced coffee flavoured milk once, by mistake: I thought it was chocolate.

"Might need this with it," said Mr Fielding and pushed a bag of raw sugar towards me. I added a teaspoonful to my coffee and had another sip. As soon as he'd gone back to the sink, I added three more.

Is her Royal Highness awake?" Mr Fielding, still scrutinising the paper, didn't bother looking up.

"Nope."

"Where's the cake you spent all yesterday afternoon baking?"

"We took it next door."

Mr Fielding didn't look very pleased. Maybe cake, not muesli, was his favourite breakfast.

"You girls will look like blimps if you keep eating like that."

I didn't know whether to titter or not. Was Mr Fielding kidding around again? I couldn't tell with him. There was a plate of toast on the bench, thick and oozing with peanut butter. He nodded to it and I took a piece. The peanut butter glued itself to the roof of my mouth and made it difficult to speak. I looked around me: here I am in the kitchen having breakfast with the father of the coolest girl in the whole school.

Chapter 8

The following Monday, I watched Natasha nibble on a carrot stick. There were several more in her Tupperware container and they represented lunch. Last Friday it was green apples; pineapple the day before. Natasha was on a single food diet.

"It's really, really great. I get to eat as much as I want, see? It just has to be the same thing all day." She crunched happily into another stick.

I folded out the cling wrap surrounding my sandwich. It was Vegemite and lettuce; the same as yesterday and the day before. I had Vegemite every day, except for when I ate peanut butter. We also had a piece of home-made cake. My favourite? Banana cake, but we usually had sultana cake because my dad liked them best. My sister traded hers as soon as she got to school for a good spot in the handball line or a Twix. I finished my sandwich and cake, but was still a bit peckish. It wouldn't do to admit it, though.

Emma and Lindsay were also on diets so eating their non-existent food wasn't an option anyway. I had no money. Mum didn't believe in wasting it on the canteen. She'd kill me if I spent my emergency money on chicken nuggets.

The other girls were proud of how little they'd eaten at lunch.

"I reckon I've had half a carrot. Tops," said Emma, running her hand over her flat stomach. "I'm going to get a three centimetre thigh gap if it kills me."

"That's great, Emms," said Lindsay. "You're already looking skinnier."

"Do you really think so, Linds. Thanks, but I'm still fat."

"No you're not," said Lindsay, after a quick glance at her own longer, thinner legs. "I've got to go. Mrs Carter is making me rewrite my science hypothesis. She needs to get a life. She's so uptight."

"I'll come with you," said Emma. "I want to sign us all up for netball tryouts."

I eyed their disappearing backs. Were they for real? I couldn't be sure. I balled up my cling wrap.

"On average, how often do you think about dieting?"

"All the time," said Natasha.

"Seriously? Why?"

"Fat thighs," said Natasha, pushing the lid on her plastic box with her thumbs.

"Your legs aren't fat."

"I've got fat arms, too."

"You haven't."

"Have, too."

For a while I stared at our out-stretched legs, hers long and brown; mine, well, average. I mean, as far as I was concerned Natasha was perfect: clear skin, Barbie blue eyes, great figure and shiny hair. But she didn't see it that way.

Her dad sure didn't help. As great as he was and everything, he sometimes called Natasha fat and told her off for eating too much. Natasha laughed it off, but watching her eat her salad ingredients like a rabbit, I figured it got to her.

The sound of the bell hauled us off the bitumen and towards the metal bin beside the tennis court. I dropped in my cling wrap and the peel of a mandarin amongst the banana skins, Oak containers and abandoned sandwiches.

I had extension maths and had just about reached the classroom when I heard someone call out my name. It was Ms Carlton, the head of the English department.

"Didn't you hear me? I've been shouting at you from across the playground. You've won a provisional place on the debating team. Congratulations. I thought you did a great job at last week's trials." She beamed at me. "Your final point about individuality went straight for the jugular." We'd been debating whether school uniforms were good or bad. She stopped, waiting, I supposed, for me to say something like "wow" or "thank you" but I didn't. I knew where this was leading and I didn't like it one bit. That was the old me. After a pause, she went on:

"I want you to come to practice this afternoon and prepare for this Friday night's debate against Northcote Boys Grammar." Just what the new me didn't want to hear. I felt myself droop.

She was gone before I could tell her that I was far too busy these days to join the boring debating team. She probably wouldn't have believed me anyway. My new school was big on debating and it was compulsory to try out for the team each year in a competition called the Art of Rhetoric. Each year's team, consisting of about six girls, went up against other schools on the first Friday of every month.

Well, at least it wasn't chess, the most clichéd nerd club of the lot. But I felt gloomy at the inevitable contempt I'd get from Natasha and the others when they asked me why I wasn't walking to the station with them. The only thing to do was keep it a secret.

Natasha texted me in geography telling me to meet her at her locker this afternoon because she had something to tell me. Phones in the classroom were forbidden so, after a quick check that the teacher was occupied with the Smart Board, I slid my phone onto my lap and returned a text that said I couldn't, that my mum was picking me up so we could go somewhere straight after school. When my phone remained silent I knew I should have sacrificed my debating session. Now Natasha was mad with me and I'd never find out her secret.

As I headed along the walkway towards room 314 after lessons I could see Emma and Lindsay leaning against Natasha's locker and talking in loud voices while she packed her bag. I heard my name and laughter, saw Natasha swinging her arm around. She wasn't imitating me playing tennis, was she? No way. Friends didn't make fun of each other's failings. I sped up and when I got to room 314 threw my bag into the corner and sat glowering on a stool up the back. I'd slipped back down the social ladder thanks to Ms Carlton. Unaware of my smoldering heart, Ms Carlton waved me down to the front.

"As you all know, Hannah had to drop out of the team because of glandular fever. I've asked Lucy Johnson to join us this week. Thank you, Lucy, for stepping in so gracefully." The girls clapped enthusiastically. I scowled. Oh, yeah. I was being really graceful about it. It's just that this was just about the worst thing that could have happened.

"This week's debate will be a tough one. Northcote Boys beat us last time. But only just. Our arguments were every bit as good as their team's. We lost on the last point."

The topic we had to practise was that a woman's place is in the home. We were the affirmative. The boys were going to argue the negative. That'd be interesting. Despite myself, I became absorbed in the preparation, helping to come up with our definition and material.

Mum and Dad were proud, of course. They always were about things like debating and chemistry competitions. Unfortunately, Dad's idea of support was to wear his lucky cap to our performances or ceremonies – even if we were just trees in the background – and tell everybody afterwards in a loud shout that we were his daughters and what a chip off the old block we were. There was no way he could be there on Friday afternoon in front of a whole boys' school. I had to shut him down.

"I'm getting a lift with Ms Carlton," I said as soon as I told him that I was in the debating team this Friday and he started his victory chicken dance.

I was all kinds of nervous on Friday afternoon: sick in my stomach, sweaty palms and a superglue mouth.

"Look in the glove compartment," said Ms Carlton when she saw the state of me. "I have some Tic Tacs."

While I was poking around for them, I came across a copy of *I Capture the Castle*. She noticed and said, "A good book with a lovely voice and sense of place. Borrow it and tell me if you agree."

"Okay. Thanks," I said, and slipped it into my blazer pocket.

We had to pick up Josie Archer and Ashleigh Bennett and, as they slid around on the back seat, Josie talked about the plot of *Riverdale* like it was for real. I stared out the window, and sucked on my Tic Tac. I'd never been to Northcote Boys Grammar before, but I knew that's where we were the moment fancy brass gates with the school crest over the top came into view. Then it dawned on me. This was where Sam and Hugh Curtis and Nick Hall went to school. What if they were there?

It was totally stupid, but in all the preparation for this debate, I hadn't given a moment's thought about the opposing team and who might be in it.

When I saw Sam, he was standing to one side of the stage, one hand in his pocket the other trying to smooth his slightly damp hair, unruly ends almost to his collar and at odds with his studious wire-framed glasses. Hey, I never knew he wore glasses. He actually looked all right in them, too, more serious, less wayward.

As soon as he saw me, he came over even though I was in a group of girls that stared at him the whole time.

"Hi, Lucy."

"Hi."

"I didn't know you'd be here tonight," Sam said.

"Neither did I, until a few days ago," I said.

"What number are you?" he asked.

"Three. You?"

"I'm going first."

"Are you nervous?" I asked him.

"Not really. Well, kind of."

"I am. I've never done this before. In front of a whole lot of people, anyway."

"Trick is to imagine them all in their underwear." Then, when he saw my face, he added, "Here, have some chocolate. It will help." He held out a little roll of Cadbury chocolate.

I shook my head.

"There's a glass and a half in every block. Think of all that calcium," he said.

"I'm on the peppermints. I'd better not mix my stimulants," I said.

He nodded, "I get it."

"I've heard your team is good."

"Yeah, we are," he said.

"Modest, too," I said. But I laughed. He laughed, too, and then half jogged back to his team. As I stood up to speak I imagined Sam and his team in their boxers and my mouth twitched. Then I thought of Sam imagining *me* in my underwear and I nearly passed out.

We lost.

And, after the debate, I had to agree with him. His team wiped the floor with us. "Don't despair, girls. This is all good practice. The important thing is not to give up," said Ms Carlton, breaking the silence in her steamy hatchback as she drove us home.

"We have something the boys don't have."

Oh yeah? "Like what, Ms Carlton?" I said.

"Girl power."

When I got home, a text from Natasha was waiting for me.

R U Free 2Morrow nite? Oval party.

Chapter 9

I'm going to the oval tonight. I'm going to the oval tonight.

It was the song in my head when I woke on Saturday morning and kept playing as I lay in bed picturing myself there and marvelling at the fact that Natasha had asked me over to her place beforehand.

What would it be like? What would I wear? Who would I talk to? What would I say? In my mind, I heard myself telling a cat joke that nobody laughed at and I felt a stabbing pain in my guts. Groaning, I clutched my stomach and rolled over onto my side facing the wall. Who'd have thought being part of the A-crowd would be so tough on the internal organs.

After a while, my eyes focused on my biology assignment stuck on the wall with Blu-Tack. It was nearly finished. All I had left to do was to write a conclusion and label the photographs that illustrated the key moments of the experiment. I grabbed a sharpie and twiddled it in my hand. I wouldn't use a sharpie, though, too boring. I needed a pen with glitter. Mum would have to drive me to the local shops.

Milly was doing handstands in the hall outside my room and leaving dirty great footprints on the wall.

"Where's Mum?" I asked her. She didn't answer.

"Mum's gonna kill you for that," I said.

"Mum's not even here," Milly righted herself. "She's next door. Mrs Wainright's gone and locked herself out again."

But when she returned, Mum was too busy to drive me.

"I have to start the dinner. You'll have to walk. Take the dogs with you. Sid especially needs a walk, he's getting fat," she said. "Don't roll your eyes at me, young lady. I don't like this new habit of yours one bit. If you want me to give you money for a pen, you have to do something for me. And I want you to walk the dogs."

Out on the street, Nancy wouldn't budge and I had to carry her most of the way. Some exercise.

I tied the dogs outside the shops and went inside, past an upright fan that blew out silver tape along with the air and straight to the rows and rows of lead pencils with sharpened ends, opposite the shiny magazines stacked in neat piles full of promises. This week's *New Scientist* was out. I picked it up and flicked through the pages. I had to be careful; the manager didn't like people touching the merchandise. I breathed in the inky printed page and admired the pictures of extinct animals newly imagined, dark matter and beautiful DNA spirals. I put it back down. I'd buy it next time, when I had more money.

I turned to face the rack of pens. As I did, the edge of my blazer swept a box of red, green and gold glitter cylinders to the floor.

Damn you, sleeve. I scrabbled for them, stretching for one that was disappearing under the shelf, my butt sticking up into the air. Ha, got 'em. I pushed my hair out of my eyes to see Nick Hall, his tie loose as usual and the shape of an iPhone heavy in his top pocket, standing in the doorway. My stomach dropped like an elevator.

Act natural. I smoothed myself down and prepared to pay at the counter. But as I tugged at my money it caught in my pocket. Flustered, I left my pen on the counter and tripped on the square carpet as I went back for it. What a klutz.

"Hey, it's Lucy, isn't it?" Nick Hall was holding my pen.

I gasped. How did he know my name? He frowned. "You catch the train with Natasha Fielding, don't you?"

"Yep." I took the pen, backed up and slipped on the step. I regained my balance and fled. A few seconds later, I stopped, mentally slapping my forehead. I had forgotten the dogs. I turned back and there was Nick Hall, crouching next to Sid, patting him.

"What's his name?"

"Sid." I slid to my knees on the pavement on the other side of Sid, gave him a kiss, murmuring, "I can't believe I forgot you, I'm so sorry," before fumbling to untie him and then Nancy. In the end I got their leads free. I was very aware of the boy beside me. We stood at the same time.

"What kind of dog are they? They look like sausage dogs."

"They're dachshunds."

"Sick," said Nick. "You're new around here."

"Kind of. I mean, I've been living in Western Australia but originally from Sydney. New to Northcote Girls, though," I said.

There was silence. I suppose he was waiting for me to ask him a question. But I couldn't think of a thing. My heart banged against my ribcage. He began to fiddle with his ear buds – which were skulls, I noticed – and his song play list.

"Well, uh, thanks." I tugged at Sid. He refused to budge. I glared at Sid, said to Nick: "Want a dog? He's going cheap."

Nick laughed. "I wish. We live in an apartment." He stooped and gave him another pat. Sid licked him. I nearly fainted. Sid decided to walk.

"Bye, little guy," Nick said.

"Maybe I'll see you at the oval tonight," I called after him. But he'd already put in his ear buds in and was strolling away, his head moving in time to the beat.

I practically had a date with Nick Hall. And, lying in bed later that night, I could still see Nick's face and the way his chin dimpled when he smiled. When I fell asleep I dreamed about being Mrs Nick Hall and living in a two-storey terrace in Paddington with a balcony and a scruffy dog staring down between the iron rails at passersby who all glanced sideways with envy. A place where the front door was always propped open by an old dictionary and three kids – two boys, mini versions of their father with brooding brown eyes and a girl, a smart little kid with straight pigtails – would be galloping up and down the hallway with bug catchers and butterfly nets in their hands. I was in the kitchen, baking biscuits after a satisfying day at work in my modernist laboratory nearby. Nick came home later with a bunch of peonies in his hand. He gave me a long passionate kiss across the stone bench and told me for the millionth time how lucky he was. I put the flowers in a vase while he swung his children, one by one, on to his shoulders to go on a bear hunt or whatever. Then, we all went out for dinner.

Chapter 10

Don't ask me why, but I said nothing about the fact that I'd run into Nick earlier that morning. Natasha had other things on her mind, anyway. I saw this the moment I arrived at her house at 5.

Simone let me in. She was wearing leggings and ugg boots and a long T-shirt that slipped off one shoulder.

"Oh, it's you," she said in a way that suggested she had been expecting someone else. Lindsay or Emma? She waved her arm towards the rear of the house, "Natasha's that way, in the kitchen," and returned to her bedroom and her iPhone.

"What are you doing?"

"Looking for candles," she said, not looking up from the drawer her head was buried in.

"Why?"

"I want to create a romantic mood. Help me look."

I opened a cupboard. Inside were a whole lot of platters.

"Why?"

"Tonight's very special. I've invited Hugh over before we go to the oval and he's going to ask me."

I opened another cupboard: tea towels and an old toaster. "Ask you what?"

"To be his girlfriend."

"Girlfriend?" I repeated.

"Der. He really likes me."

"I know," I said. "I can tell."

"Can you? How? Tell me everything," said Natasha, shutting the drawer hard and swinging round. "Did he say something to you? Did Sam?"

"Well, no. I just meant that I've seen the way he looks at you all the time."

Natasha resumed her work of setting up for a romantic scene and I felt disappointed. Somehow, I'd let her down.

"Is Simone going out?" I peered into another cupboard and saw plates, big and small.

She rolled her eyes, of course. "When isn't Simone going out?" She picked up a saucer and examined it thoughtfully, "she has a new boyfriend. Hmmm, do you think this would make a good candle holder?"

"Perfect." I imagined the room filled with the seductive glow of candles. I then had a thought. "Your dad? Won't he, like, spoil the mood of seduction?"

"Dad?" Natasha moved a cushion a little to the right. "I've made him promise to stay in his room. Look, are you helping or not?"

By the time the doorbell rang at 7.30, Natasha was dressed in a cute pair of shorts and tight T-shirt over a push-up bra. Her hair was out. She'd melted the bottom of several candles and rammed them onto saucers I had pulled out of the cupboard and arranged on the windowsill and side table. She had also draped a nylon pink shawl over a lamp and brought out all the pillows and cushions from the bedroom. The effect was that of a boudoir.

Hugh must have got the message because he was soon sitting on the Fielding couch with Natasha's feet across his lap. His arm rested on her legs which she'd draped across his lap, her hair was an attractive tangle against a round teal cushion. She leaned in and kissed him on his ear. Somehow, without him even asking, they'd become an item. Going together to the oval later, would be, I guessed, like making a general public announcement.

The doorbell rang. I could hear Sam's voice in the hallway. He was telling Mr Fielding a joke that went on and on because Sam kept pausing to crack up. Mr Fielding used one of his pauses to escape to his bedroom and slam the door. Undaunted, Sam delivered the punch line through the keyhole, before making his way into the sitting room.

"I don't think he got the joke," he said, and then, looking round, "This looks just like a sultan's tent or a genie's bottle or something. What's going on?" Natasha gave Sam one of her withering looks that would have worked on me.

"I don't recall inviting you?"

"Hugh did." Sam didn't appear to take offence. There was no room for him on the couch and the other chairs were covered in papers and piles of clothes waiting for ironing so he just stood there. Shouldn't Natasha offer him a chair? I glanced at her. Maybe I should. But before I could move, Sam spied a chair in the kitchen and dragged it across the room.

"You might want to ask first." Natasha sounded annoyed. Sam sat down anyway. The chair, I saw, was coming apart at the base. Oh shit. I held my breath. Bamm. Sam fell through the chair. He didn't move at first and his face was all twisted like he was in pain. Hugh didn't bother to see if he was okay. Didn't even look. No brotherly concern, there. Natasha leaned forward to check he was all right.

"Do you mind not breaking my furniture?"

"I'm all right. No need for alarm." Sam's tone was sarcastic and I didn't blame him. At least he was okay. Sam stood and picked up the broken chair.

Hugh turned on the television and moved to the front of the couch, his knees almost touching the screen. "Shut up," he said mildly. Australia was playing the West Indies. His hair flopped forward. He pushed it back and turned up the volume. Really, it was a very nice strong arm – probably from all the cricket he played. I liked how brown it was and how he'd rolled his sleeves up to his elbow, like he was about to get down to it, although what *it* was, I didn't really know.

Natasha jumped up and padded out to the kitchen. I followed her and stood beside her to look through the window.

"Do you think your dad will be mad about the chair?"

She poured a glass of water. She shrugged. I got a glass of water and took a sip.

"Are you okay?" I asked after a while.

"Why wouldn't I be?"

"No reason. You seem annoyed, is all. Is it because Sam broke the chair? Or have I done something?"

Natasha didn't answer. I could hear Hugh and Sam talking under the noise of the television. I said: "Do you still want to go to the oval?"

She said: "I've been thinking. You should go out with Sam. You need a boyfriend."

"I don't think he likes me that way." I let down my glass, but didn't let go of it straightaway. I didn't tell her that if I was going to get a boyfriend, I wanted it to be Nick Hall. She gave me a long stare and I felt my face turning red. Could she tell I liked Nick?

"Maybe," she said. "But it would be totally great if we were dating brothers."

"So, Hugh's asked you then?"

"Not exactly. But we're definitely a couple."

"Will we go to the oval now?"

"Not yet. Let's play a game." She led me back to the living room. I wondered what sort. Monopoly? In my family, I was quite the property mogul.

"Guys. Stop watching TV. It's boring. Let's play something."

"Like what?" Sam and Hugh both stared at Natasha.

"Let's play Truth or Dare."

Neither boy spoke. Frankly, they looked about as horrified as me.

Natasha stood over Hugh, leaned down and took his hand. He pulled her to him. She went with it, saying, "It will be so much fun. You'll see."

He moved his mouth close to her ear, said something that I couldn't hear. It made Natasha slowly smile, eyes half closed.

"Okay. Let's get this party started." Natasha pulled herself up, shook her hips in a figure eight. Hugh's eyes practically popped out of his head. She skipped away, giggling, and went back into the kitchen. I could hear the clink of glasses and cupboards opening. I followed her back and whispered: "What about your dad?"

"What he doesn't know won't hurt him." She nudged my shoulder with hers, two drinks full to the brim in her hands. "Here, try this," she pushed a drink into my hand.

I lifted the glass up to my lips to sip it and just about spat it out.

"Crap, Natasha. What's in it?"

"Just orange juice … and a smidgen of vodka." Her eyes challenged me. I wanted to smack her, I really did. Leave, at least. Instead, I banged down the cup.

Natasha's eyes rolled: "You are way too uptight, Lucy. Don't make me regret asking you over instead of Lindsay."

I sighed. "Just let me know next time, okay?"

Natasha's smile was just a flicker. She handed over my drink, and another, "Here, give these to the guys. I'll make you something special."

Sam gave me a funny look when I brought him a drink. God, what if he thinks I like him? I sat as far away from him as I could, on the edge of the couch with my knees firmly together, sipping my new drink, which was, if anything, stronger. I snuck a peek at Natasha's drink. It was nearly empty. So were the boys' drinks. I tipped my head back – down the hatch. I lowered the glass and examined its level. Still more than half-full. The effort made my eyes water, but eventually it was gone. I set down my glass on the table, feeling quite normal. After all, I could see perfectly. And then after a while I couldn't. Another funny thing was, I couldn't feel my toes. I wriggled them. I looked up and noticed that everyone was laughing, even Hugh. What was so funny? Was it me? I put my hair behind my ears. Then I realised that I was listing to the left. I pushed myself upright and tried to say sorry, but it didn't come out right. I hiccupped, once, twice. I tried to hold my breath to stop them.

"Look everyone. Lucy's tipsy already," Natasha laughed.

"Am not." I hiccupped.

"Quick, give her a glass of water."

I sipped on the water and collected myself. I felt all light-headed and happy. Confident, too, like I could do anything, be anyone. It was a delirious feeling. I smiled at my new friends and wasn't at all perturbed when Natasha suggested that we start playing.

"I'll go first," she said, her voice breathy with anticipation. "I pick dare."

"I dare you to get a cumquat from that crazy guy's backyard, Mr Hollis, or whatever his name is," said Sam.

She pretended to crack her knuckles – "*That's so easy*" – and was gone.

While we waited, Sam and I played a game of thumb wars. "Best of three," said Sam as he squashed my thumb about 30 seconds into the first game. I twisted my thumb left and right until I fell off the couch. "Aww," I said, rubbing my head.

"Go easy on her, Sam," said Hugh.

"I didn't know you cared," I said, looking deeply into his eyes, thinking, "Damn, flirting is too *easy*."

He stretched his legs out in front of him and leaned back.

"I don't."

I pretended to pout until his girlfriend appeared at the glass, still barefoot triumphantly holding a cumquat aloft and swaying in a victory dance. Hugh's eyes followed her every move.

She pulled open the door and sashayed in.

"I deserve something special for that."

"And I'm going to give it to you," said Hugh and he pulled her onto his lap and put his arms around her waist. She put her head into his neck then twisted to tell Sam it was his turn. He shook himself slightly and stretched his neck from side to side.

"Dare."

Natasha's eyes sparkled and she said slowly: "I dare you to kiss Lucy." I could feel him tense up beside me and he gave Natasha a nasty look. Then he shrugged. "No problem." He made to kiss me. Huh? I shrank back.

"Don't be shy, Lucy. It's just a kiss," said Natasha. "Go into another room if you have to."

"Here's fine," I said quickly. Sam leaned forward and put one on my cheek.

"Pathetic. That's not a dare," said Natasha scornfully. "You have to go into the laundry for, I don't know, two minutes. And no cheating: you have to kiss."

I stood up, wobbling a bit on my legs, and threaded my way into the laundry. Sam pulled a goofy face and followed. When the door closed behind us, he said. "We don't have to kiss. They won't know the difference."

We stood, breathing heavily, waiting it out, until I pressed him against the Fielding's top loader and kissed him, hard on the lips. Sam didn't respond straightaway. I started to draw back, confused. A row of shirts waiting to be ironed, brushed against our heads. He said, quickly: "Hey, where are you going?" and pulled me back. We kissed again. I became aware of his hand under my T-shirt – second base – and anticipation and fear uncoiled in the base of my stomach. Just as I was sinking down, a bag of rags dropped down from the shelf above onto Sam's head. We sprang apart, Sam knocking over a pile of washing, and we spilled out of the laundry, tangled in socks and T-shirts reeking of fabric softener.

Sam flung himself on the couch without looking at me. "It's someone else's turn now."

"Lucy's," said Natasha, slyly. I felt a rush of warmth to my cheeks. Will this never end?

A tingle of something weird went through me. I put my arms across my middle. "I don't feel very well."

She ignored me, chanted: "Truth or Dare, Truth or Dare?"

"I think I'm going to be sick ..." I made it as far as the doorway to the kitchen before upending the contents of my stomach.

That put a stop to the game in any case. It also meant we weren't going to the oval. She was impatient as she helped me into the bathroom so that I could clean my teeth and go to the toilet.

I managed to crawl to the bedroom and lay on the top of my bed. The room was spinning and I couldn't see how to make it stop.

"You can still go to the oval. I'll be fine here," I said.

"Hugh doesn't want to go anymore." She disappeared into her wardrobe and returned in a bright-green T-shirt for bed. I could see two of her so I half closed one eye. On it was a picture of a worm coming out of an apple.

"You're cleaning up your own mess in the morning," she said as she climbed into bed. "I don't do vomit."

She turned away from me and soon her breathing became regular. I continued to lie on my back. Every time I shut my eyes the bed tried to buck me off so I focused on the moon through the window. It was a throbbing grey pumice stone. My mouth was dry. Should I get up and fetch a glass of water from the bathroom? I'd never make it, I thought. Better just to go to sleep.

Chapter 11

The following morning, while Natasha was in the shower, I flopped on the plastic rattan lounge on the back deck hoping the fresh air would help my queasy stomach. Inside, in the kitchen, I could hear Simone and Mr Fielding arguing.

"What time do you call that?" shouted Mr Fielding. It was followed by a storm of melodramatic weeping. I covered my ears. My head throbbed. If this was what being hungover felt like, I couldn't understand why so many people raved about getting wasted.

"Good morning." I squinted up at the shadow of Sam's head. His ears glowed red in the morning sunlight behind him. I covered my eyes.

"How are you feeling?"

"Fine if I don't look at you and you don't shout so loud."

"Can I sit down?"

"If you have to." But I scooted over.

He settled down beside me. "Where's Natasha?"

"Having a shower. Hugh?"

"Cricket practice."

"Natasha said he was mad at me."

"What for?"

Everything. A checkerboard shadow from the lattice roof blurred our faces, making me feel sick again.

"Too bright for you?" said Sam, in a teasing voice.

I groaned. "How bad was I? Natasha's not talking to me."

"Not too bad, except at the end. Why are there always carrots in vomit?"

Vomit. Oh, God. "Are you sad we didn't go to the oval?"

Sam stared into the middle distance. "Nah."

Was he for real? I glanced his way and caught his grin.

"Reckon it was more fun here," he said.

"Thanks. I think." I rested a bare foot on the wooden framework of the balustrade. "I'm not very good at being drunk."

"Oh, I don't know, better than being a lush."

I felt myself cringe at the thought of being a lush.

"Are you all right? You look kinda funny," said Sam.

"Fine. Never better." I sat up straighter, causing fresh waves of nausea. "I have to lie down," I said weakly, and began to tip over sideways.

"No, you don't," said Sam, grabbing my arm and pushing me up. "Better to stand."

We stood facing each other, too close, his hands on either side of my forearms until I was steady. I noticed that his eyes were grey with green flecks. I suspected I still reeked of vomit. Shower time.

"I should go," I said. "But thanks. Thanks for everything."

Inside, I found Natasha at the kitchen bench painting her nails pale blue. She didn't look up as I sat on a stool beside her. So, still mad.

"They look nice," I said looking at her nails.

She examined them herself. "Yeah." She blew on them. "What have you been doing?"

"Nothing. Just outside with Sam," I said. "He wanted to say thanks for last night." He said nothing of the sort but I thought it might improve her mood.

Natasha pursed her lips. "Did he have a good time?"

"Said he did." That at least was true. That seemed to satisfy her. She screwed the lid back on the polish. "Did he tell you where Hugh is?"

"Cricket."

"God, he loves that game." Natasha waved her hands around. "Once these dry, I'll give him a call.

Bet you heard all that with dad and Simone." Natasha rolled her eyes. "My sister is such a drama queen."

The back door swung back. It was Sam. He stood in the doorway.

"You again," she said, but laughed to show she didn't mean it. "What do you want?"

"Want to see if, um, Lucy wants to go, like, maybe, go to the shops, get a drink or something, a Berocca, maybe. You, too, Natasha," he added politely.

"Gee, what girl could resist an offer like that," she said, sliding off her stool.

Sam's thongs made a slapping sound on the pavement as we walked, three abreast, to the corner shop. Sam whistled tunelessly on one side of Natasha. I was on the other.

"Would you stop whistling," said Natasha.

"Why are you always so mean?" said Sam, lightly.

"I am not," Natasha said. "I'm just truthful. That's good, right?"

"That's one way of looking at it. Sure." He took up whistling again. Natasha's face hardened. "So, is Lucy a good kisser?"

Sam stopped whistling. I practically stopped breathing. "Natasha!" Natasha smirked and shoved Sam with her shoulder. "At least that shut him up."

Sam shoved back. "No way." He put his hands in his pockets and started whistling again.

"So, you're saying Lucy's not a good kisser?"

I gave him a death stare. How dare he think I wasn't a good kisser.

He held up his hands, placatingly, "That's not what I'm saying at all. I just don't think it's cool to kiss and tell."

"So, in other words, the answer's no." Natasha sounded triumphant.

My head throbbed. I covered my ears. "Shut up. Everyone just stop talking."

"And whistling," said Natasha, looking pointedly at Sam.

We had arrived at the automatic doors of Seven Eleven. Sam started to head inside. "Coming?"

Now that we were here, I couldn't seem to bring myself to go inside. The morning was already warm and I could feel the prickle of sweat – and humiliation – inside my clothes. Sam thinks I'm a hopeless kisser.

"Stay outside, no problem," he said. "Tell me what you want?" But I didn't know that either.

Sam looked enquiringly at Natasha.

"A Paddle Pop. Definitely," she said.

"Lucy?"

"Okay," I said glumly.

"What flavor?"

"I'm having chocolate," said Natasha. "She's got to have chocolate. It's the best."

I nodded even though everyone in my family knew for a fact that I only ever ate banana Paddle Pops.

"Chocolate it is," and Sam disappeared inside.

We took our ice creams further down the street to a handkerchief-sized park on the edge of the nearly empty car park.

"Did you know our schools are having an informal together next week?" Natasha delicately touched the tip of her tongue to her mouth to catch a drip.

"Yup," said Sam. His legs dangled over the side of the table and one of his thongs came off, dropping into the dust. He hooked it back up with his foot all the while keeping his eyes on the guys on skateboards dropping figure eights in spaces between the solitary cars.

"It's compulsory for all Year 10."

"Same here."

"Great."

I realised something. "Hugh won't be there. He's in Year 11."

"Nope." "Yep." Natasha and Sam spoke at the same time.

"It's cool," said Natasha, airily. "The girls are coming over beforehand to do hair and make-up at mine. It'll be a blast. Right, Lucy?"

"Right," I said, even though I didn't have a clue what she was talking about.

"That's cool." Sam threw his ice cream stick at the bin and missed. Natasha looked past him.

"Hey, isn't that Nick Hall? From your brother's year?" We squinted at the skateboarders.

There he was, a tall figure with his long dark fringe and black denim jeans lounging against the bus stop wall, his left foot resting on a skateboard and pushing it, backwards and forwards.

"Yep," said Sam. "That's Nick."

Natasha looked interested. "Oh, yeah?" She slid him another look, slipped off the table and slowly walked over to the bin nearest to the parking ticket machine. She dropped the stick into it, half smiled at him, before turning around and strolling back. Nick Hall, leaning against the wall and looking cool doing it, pretended he didn't notice. But his eyes were on Natasha just the same.

Mr Fielding was in the front yard when we got home.

"Your boyfriend has been looking for you," he said.

Natasha frowned prettily. He pointed to their back door.

"Inside, girls. I want a cup of coffee."

I followed them inside, but Sam backed away. "See you."

Crumbs and papers littered every surface of the kitchen, and there was a tower of mugs and breakfast bowls in the sink. Natasha made a half-hearted attempt to look for the dishcloth, wrinkling her nose when she found it in last night's baking tray.

"Gross, Dad. Can't you ever clean up?"

"Not my job, Einstein. I was the cook. Remember?"

"What do you mean? I made your breakfast." Natasha, nonetheless, started demolition on the crockery tower. Mr Fielding disappeared for a moment and then stumped back into the room, tucking a fresh denim shirt into his chinos and ignoring me.

"Is my coffee ready?"

Natasha had lined up three cups under the spout, then poured in hot foamy milk. She then pulled out a Sara Lee chocolate cake box minus its cardboard lid from the fridge.

"Dad loves chocolate cake. Don't you, Dad?" said Natasha, pretending to pull away the cake when he reached for a second piece. For the first time that morning she looked happy.

"Look what happens when you don't make cakes for your old man. He turns to another woman. Sara Lee."

Natasha cut a few pieces and took a piece for herself before sliding the foil container over to Mr Fielding. Straight away, Mr Fielding took two more pieces. Between bites he said to her, "I wouldn't eat that if I were you."

"Very funny, Dad," said Natasha, but she put down her piece. Mr Fielding then asked when I thought I was going home. "You don't live here, you know."

His words stung. What should I say? Yes? No? Turn it into a joke: Say "Oh, I thought I did live here."

I wished he wouldn't do that: be all jokey one minute then say something like that. Natasha kept swatting crumbs from the bench. I couldn't tell if she agreed with her dad or not. No, I wouldn't risk it. I texted Mum to pick me up.

Chapter 12

It turned out Mr Fielding was kidding. Or at least that's what I decided because the following Saturday, the night of the combined Northcote Grammar schools informal, he had offered to take us and he wouldn't have done that if he thought I was a bad influence. There was a catch, though.

Brigitte rang just before I left for Natasha's with a bag full of make-up and my dress.

"Hey, Dad'll pick you up at six. Okay?"

Thunk. I slapped my head with the heel of my hand. I'd forgotten I'd agreed to a lift with Brigitte's dad.

"Are you there? Lucy?"

"I'm here," I said. "Ahhh, sorry, Briggy. I forgot all about it. But, see, I'm getting a lift with Natasha. She's going to do my hair and make-up beforehand."

There was the sound of hurt silence. I quickly filled it, "But I'll see you there, right? We'll, you know, dance together, and stuff."

"Sure. Okay, no problem," and Brigitte was gone.

Shit.

As soon as I arrived at Natasha's, though, I forgot to feel bad.

"Simone's hair tongs are already on. Let's do this thing," said Natasha, all business-like, and leading me straight to the bathroom where she'd laid out a towel on which she'd arranged mascaras and brushes and other tools, eyeshadows and pots of lip gloss. These were mostly Simone's, she informed me. "But she's out and what she doesn't know won't hurt her."

And she proceeded to straighten, curl and paint me for what seemed like hours. "You're going to be hot AF when I've finished with you," she crooned.

But when I looked at myself in the mirror, I nearly had a heart attack. I had never worn so much make-up in all my life. Natasha stood beside me at the mirror.

"So, do you love it? You look gorgeous. Sam is going to totally freak out when he sees you."

The door bell rang and a few seconds later Emma and Lindsay trouped in.

"Holy crap. Lucy looks like a ho," said Emma, pulling up in the doorway with a look of horror.

"Don't say that!" I moaned. I collapsed on the toilet seat and put my head between my knees.

"Now look what you've done," said Natasha.

"Sorry," said Emma. "Lucy, she's made your eyes really stand out."

"I need a paper bag," I said.

"What? To put over your head?" Emma said.

Lindsay punched her arm as a warning. "It's not that bad. Truly."

"No, to blow into," I said, weakly.

"Does that even work?" Linsday looked around at everyone. "What? I'm just curious."

"What am I going to do?" I wailed.

"Just take one of Simone's antidepressants and you'll be fine," said Natasha. "Now, go get dressed while I do someone else. Which one of you is up?"

"Me!" Emma and Lindsay spoke at the same time and almost knocked me over in the stampede to get in front of Natasha. Emma won. Lindsay fluffed her hair in the mirror while she waited.

Left to my own devices, I wrestled with my outfit – a floral dress and a belt – in an attempt to get it on without smudging my make-up.

"What are those?"

I glanced up, startled, at Lindsay, who was staring at me in wonder. "What?" I peered down at myself, saw my striped boyleg Bonds undies and beige bra. "These? They're my undergarments. Why?"

"You need to go to Victoria's Secret, honey."

"Oh, okay," I said, rearranging the dress to hide myself. "Thanks for the tip."

By now Natasha had finished with Emma and was calling for Lindsay.

"Shame the Year 11 boys won't be there, Natasha," said Emma, inserting padding into her lacy Victoria's Secret bra.

Natasha, busy with Emma, didn't answer. I noticed she was already dressed in tight white jeans, brown leather belt and white T-shirt. Hugh didn't know what he was missing.

"Someone get my phone," ordered Natasha after she'd finished with Emma and had applied smoky make-up to her own eyes. "Time to make memories," she called and sat on the edge of the bath. "And everyone else jealous." Lindsay held up her fist to Emma for a punch. Natasha laughed and held out her arm. We crowded around her. "Say 'thirsty'." She pressed for a burst. Lindsay and Emma, giggling, held their own phones up to do the same.

"Can you pass that," I said to Emma, pointing to my phone on the edge of the vanity.

"Very not glittery," she said. "I'm impressed."

"I'm so totally going to upload this." Natasha showed us her selection. Natasha's arm was around my shoulder. She looked beautiful and, beside her, I looked like a possum caught in headlights, all big-eyed and freaked out, my hair standing on end.

Natasha kissed our reflections goodbye in the mirror. "Let's go, bitches," and turned her back on the frosted shape of her mouth against the glass.

Natasha's dad left us to cluster at the bottom of the stairs up to the gym hall of Northcote Boys Grammar School. Music and the scent of Lynx mingled in the air as we edged past a group of boys into a queue to put our phones into ziplock bags with our names printed out in black permanent marker and then into the lockers for safekeeping.

"Betcha don't know who it is?" and a pair of hands covered my eyes. I pulled them off and twisted to see who it was.

"Oh, it's you."

"Don't sound so disappointed." Sam put his weight on one foot and then the other. He gestured to the boy standing beside him. "My friend here is Paul. This is Lucy and Natasha and … sorry I don't remember your names."

"Emma," said Emma.

"Lindsay," said Lindsay

Both sounded a little put out that Sam hadn't known their names.

"Pleased to meet ya." Paul was solid and sure of himself in jeans, a button-down shirt, a curly flat-top and a smile that revealed tiny incisors. Over his left shoulder, I saw a teacher in a rumpled brown suit glowing like a Geiger counter under the green exit light monitoring the procession to the toilets. I tugged at Natasha.

"I need to, you know, go to the toilet. Coming?"

"Nah."

"Oh, okay," I said, surprised. I was used to Brigitte who liked to do everything together which, if I thought about it was a bit, you know, tweenie.

"I'll come," said Emma. "I want to find out how you know these guys." She hoisted up her bag and pulled a little at her tight dress.

"Hang on, Lucy." It was Sam.

"I'll take you."

"We're fine," I said.

"I'll get into trouble with old Poncy. That guy over there, Ponsonby. We're supposed to escort our guests." His voice rose at the end and took on a plummy tone and he sort of laughed. Emma giggled, swept at her hair in a flirty way and batted her eyelashes.

"Oh, sure," I said. But at the toilet door, I stopped. "You don't have to wait for us."

"Nah, probably not," said Sam. But when we pushed open the bathroom door he was still there, a few feet away, kicking at the wall and talking to a couple of guys. "Later. I'd better, you know ..." He tipped his head in our direction, the boys looking us over as Sam escorted us back to the dance floor.

There we stood, playing it cool, on the edge, which was bare except for the dancing light from a disco ball. I could see Natasha in the centre of a group. Paul was sort of hopping around in front of her. I guess you'd call it dancing and the jagged tears in his jeans looked white beneath the strobes. Bees to honey. How does she do it? Natasha was good looking with her flawless skin and her smile that could clean up a room. But it was more than that. Somehow, she was *right* looking. You know? Her hair was the perfect shade of blonde, catching the light warmly and cut in an effortless but not unruly style. No frizz for her. She had exactly the right amount of tan, warm enough to make her appear healthy, but not too much that she looked like an old wrinkled boot. Her figure was perfect, and so were her clothes. Her white jeans hit just the right note, too. Blue denim would have been much too casual. There was no sign of my pendant, but she wore just the right amount of thin silver bangles that tinkled when she moved, but weren't try-too-hard. But there was something else, too. What was it? I searched around for the little thing. Appeal? Confidence? I couldn't find the right word, but whatever it was, she had it in abundance. And, boy, did she know it.

"Does Natasha even like Hugh?" Sam was asking me. Huh? I swung around to take him in. Emma was listening hard, waiting for my answer. Funny, how all of a sudden I was an expert on Natasha.

"Um, yeah," I said. "Course. Why?"

"Just wondering." Something in his tone made me peer at him, but his face was shadowed enough for me not catch its expression. Admiration? Brotherly concern? Before I could investigate further, he had stepped forward. "C'mon," he said, so we followed.

The night was a hectic, mysterious and exciting swirl of colour, music and movement so that I felt like I had been painted into Van Gogh's *Starry Night*. My ears throbbed as I danced, around and around and around. At one point, Sam leaned in to say, "I like your dress." But he did it in a funny way that made me laugh. Boys loomed up out of nowhere, joining in to check us out. Sam pushed them away and they'd good humouredly go back to leaning against walls. Once, when Sam and I were twisting around at the edge of the dance floor, a few of his friends came over and tried to tell me a joke. I couldn't hear half of it, but the way they kept interrupting one another and catching hold of my arm to keep my attention gave me a rush of power, the kind that girls like Natasha took for granted, but for me felt new and exciting. It was easy, then, to stop taking myself so seriously and my wild imitations of the Gangnam dance became the hit of the night. Later, a group of us found a corner where we sat with our legs crossed, knees almost touching, in a circle and talking about who'd watched *Game of Thrones* last week, who had kissed who or what about the kid who broke his collarbone coming off his skateboard at the oval last Saturday night, and how the police were called when someone set fire to the grandstand.

I eventually noticed that my knee was more than brushing against the knee next to it. I looked at the jean clad knee and then into the eyes of its owner.

"I've seen you on the station," said Paul.

"Have you?" I was surprised.

"Got a boyfriend?"

"No."

"You and Sam don't have something?" said Paul. He had turned towards me, away from the others, and kept his voice low so that I had to lean in to him in order to hear.

"Your friend over there, the good-looking one, is going out with Sam's brother, isn't she?"

I nodded.

"Do you want to go somewhere quiet?" he asked softly, touching my arm.

I shook my head. I was flattered, but something held me back.

"No worries," he said, turning away.

Chapter 13

"I haven't talked to you all night," Natasha complained as she and I were at the drinks table, choosing from an assortment of warm cans of soft drink. I wished for a bottle of water.

"Oh, sorry," I said. "I've been dancing and stuff. It's been fun."

Natasha took a slug from a can of Pepsi Max. "I told you. You look smokin' hot."

I felt gratified at that, and duly gave credit where it was due, nudging her back and saying, "Thanks to *you*."

Natasha lifted her can, "Here's to concealer."

"To M.A.C. concealer," I said, lifting my own. "You and Hugh make a good couple. Pity he's not here."

I expected her to agree so I was surprised when she just shrugged. I had to admit, even though we'd become pretty good friends over the past month, doing homework together and hanging out with the Curtis brothers, I still didn't really get her. We'd talked about stuff, everyday stuff like favourite nail polish colour (blue), movie (*The Perks of Being a Wallflower* – driving through the city standing on the back of a truck was on her bucket list) and pizza topping (Margherita), but lots of important things too. I knew that she hated her mother, for instance, and that she made a cup of coffee for her dad every morning when he woke up. She was not a morning person. I knew that, too. She didn't say much until about 9. And she knew lots about me: that my dad had lost his job in Western Australia and moved the family back to Sydney, broke, and that my Aunt Gert, our only living relative, helped out financially. That I'd sat for a scholarship at Northcote Girls in Year 7 and was really bummed out when I didn't get it (I came fourth) and we had to move away, but then I'd applied for a half scholarship for Year 10 and got it. That I'd once had a cigarette but I'd hadn't drawn back. And that I'd never had a proper boyfriend. At the same time, we sort of weren't that close and I found myself with nothing to say when we were together.

Natasha was just about to take another sip of drink when her elbow was knocked by a scuffle in the boys' queue for drinks and she splashed soft drink onto her white top.

"Hey." She gave him the finger. "Moron." She stared at her front. "I'm going to have to wash this off. Coming?"

We pushed open the door of the toilet we were pretty sure had been assigned to the girls for the night – there was a big picture of Scarlett Johansson as Black Widow on the door.

"I wonder what's on the boys' door? Thor or the Incredible Hulk?" I said before getting distracted by the stainless-steel urinals. "I wonder if Nick Hall uses these?" The thought made me breathless.

Natasha splashed water on herself.

"Do you know what I think?" Natasha was drying her T-shirt under the dryer and raised her voice over the din. "You should forget about him and go for Sam."

Not this again.

"Shhh," I said checking under the stall to make sure we were alone and there wasn't Sam or one of his friends lurking.

"Don't you want to?" Natasha switched the dryer on again.

"Umm, we're just friends."

"Yeah, well, haven't you heard of friends with benefits?"

"That's gross." But I giggled as I opened a cubicle door, "I need to pee," and shut the door with a bang.

Outside, the dryer droned to a stop. I pulled down my sensible undies and waited. In the silence, I called out, "Has it dried yet?"

She didn't answer. I flushed and opened up the door. No Natasha.

Outside, the strobe lights were pumping in time to the music and the party was in full swing. I blinked, disorientated.

"Hi, Lucy."

But it wasn't Natasha, it was Brigitte calling my name. She was hanging out with Bunny and a few others.

I was pleased to see them and hugged her. "Hey, you!"

"Hey," said Brigitte. "Having a good time? We're going to see if the DJ takes requests. Want to come?"

"I can't," I said. "I'm looking for Natasha. Have you seen her?"

Brigitte shook her head. Bunny nudged her, "Tell Lucy about the guy that fell over the chair, taking one of the teachers down with him."

"Really?"

"Yeah, you should have seen it. So funny."

We stood together a while longer until eventually the group floated away. They were all right. I liked them a lot. We used to have a lot of fun, but they were into different things. Anyway, right now I just wanted to find Natasha. I hoped she was all right.

The sight of her 15 minutes later, in the middle of a laughing group, made me feel unexpectedly mad.

I pushed through, "excuse me, excuse me", until I was standing in front of her.

"I waited ages for you. Outside the toilet. Why didn't you tell me you were going?"

"I thought I did," said Natasha. "Honestly. You mustn't have heard me."

I stared at her doubtfully. She put a hand on my arm, "As if I would have just left you there. I mean, come on."

She looked sincere and a little hurt that I could think such a thing. "Okay, well, it's just that I felt stupid talking to myself."

"It's fine." Natasha's smile was warm and forgiving and she shifted to let me in, forcing the guy – I think it was Paul – she'd been talking to before I'd interrupted to step back to make room.

The party had lost some of its lustre. Perhaps I was tired. I fought it down. This was supposed to be *fun*. I could sleep when I was dead, right? I turned to Paul and gave him my biggest smile, probably looking inane rather than alluring.

Paul grinned wolfishly back. "Where have you been all my life?"

"Right here." I hoped my laugh sounded tinkling and maybe it did because Paul held out his hand. "Let's go somewhere quiet. I'll show you the weights room."

Did I want to go with him? Not really, but I stood, anyway, and put my hand in his. We wouldn't be long and we'd just be talking. I let him lead me away.

The weights room with its frayed carpet, odd assortment of grimy dumb-bells and stale sweat smell was underwhelming.

"Nice."

Paul, who was still holding my hand, didn't notice my sarcasm. He pulled me closer.

"I'm really, really glad you're here, Lucy," he said. He kissed me on the mouth. He tasted of alcohol. I wrinkled my nose.

"Maybe we should go back to the others."

"Now that I've got you alone, I'm not letting you go." Paul kept the tone light, but kissed me again. I laughed, too, but nervously. I tried kissing him back, but it felt awkward. It didn't feel right. I pulled free and started for the door. He wrapped two arms around my waist to stop me.

"Hey, where do you think you're going?"

The sweaty carpet was making me want to gag and I withdrew from him as much as I could within the confines of his arms. But I wasn't the one in control, he was. He kissed me again, roughly this time, and his mouth was hard. I could feel his sharp teeth beneath my lips. Everything was going all weird. It was *Starry Night* out of control. I'd started out feeling flattered that he'd singled me out for attention. I felt special. I was attractive. He wanted to spend time alone with me.

Now, I felt scared. He was holding me too tightly and it was starting to hurt. I didn't want Paul to get mad at me or stop liking me or, even worse, think I was frigid or a loser. A cool girl, someone like Natasha or Lindsay, would definitely be up for it. If I pushed him away, he'd think I was immature, uptight or, even worse, a tease.

I could feel him on my throat, my neck, my lips. This time I didn't kiss back. His hands kept crawling under my dress, rubbing my thighs and stroking my behind.

Stop, I thought. But, coward that I was, I didn't speak it aloud. Paul ignored my fists pushing him away and kept at it. I could feel his hardness against my thigh, and I shuddered. But he didn't care. If anything, it made him more amorous. Tears filled my eyes. This wasn't romantic or sexy. He lifted my skirt and pushed into me further, further. This can't be happening, I thought hysterically. I gave one last shove.

Paul, without hesitation, shoved back, like I was an unwanted rag doll. But he let me go.

"We were just messing around," he said. I was confused, unsure, for that wasn't what it felt like to me.

"I want to go back to the others," I said.

"Sure thing," he said, rubbing the curl into his flat top. "Door's that way."

I ran, flinging open the door and slamming it behind me and I found myself in the bathroom again, shaking all over. I stared at myself in the mirror. I looked pale, shocked, upset. My head ached, my legs, too. I splashed water on my face and dried it with a scratchy paper towel which left tiny flecks on my cheeks. I flicked at them. Stupid, stupid. I leaned my hands on the vanity.

There I stayed until I'd counted to 10 and back again. By then my heart had stopped pounding and colour had returned to my cheeks. I looked almost normal, like nothing had ever happened. Good. Nobody could ever know. It would be humiliating. The new me was sophisticated and cool, not pathetic and frigid. I must have misread the signals. I pressed my knuckles into my eye sockets until I saw stars. I'd better go back to the group before someone came looking for me.

Sam saw me rejoin the circle next to Natasha. I tried not to look at him. "Are you all right?" he mouthed. Yes, I said, lying so well I nearly fooled myself. But a cold piece of marble sat in my stomach for the rest of the night.

Chapter 14

Things weren't right after the informal. Natasha became elusive. At school, I tried to catch her on her own, but always she was with someone else. Or I'd glimpse her on the stairs and by the time I'd reached her she'd be gone. The same thing happened at the canteen line. Once, I saw her in serious conversation with Lindsay. Wasn't Natasha supposed to be tired of Lindsay's possessiveness? Everything had gone from being perfect to being crazy and weird. Was it something I'd said? Done? My heart thumped dully. Was it something I hadn't done?

By Tuesday I was exhausted with worry. There were black circles under my eyes from not sleeping. I leaned weakly against my locker. If only Natasha would return my calls or at least answer my texts.

The prospect of double biology, usually my idea of heaven, had no appeal whatsoever.

"Good morning Lucy." Ms Carlton rounded the corner with a clipboard in her hand. "Shouldn't you be in class? Wait, now I've got you here I might as well tell you that we are merging our debating teams with Northcote Boys and taking on a couple of schools in another state. We've selected partners for you. You are with ..." She consulted her clipboard. "Sam Curtis. We'll be having a meeting all together next week to discuss strategy. He already knows you, apparently."

Good grief. Could this week get any worse? I felt sick. I touched my neck, perhaps my glands were up. Perhaps I was coming down with something.

What if Paul told Sam about me? What if he said he'd, you know, done *it* with me? What if he said he hadn't? I didn't know which was worse. I couldn't eat my Vegemite sandwich at lunchtime. My forehead felt hot against my palm. Perhaps I should visit Sick Bay, lie on a pull-out bed and sink into a coma until I was 25.

I pushed my folder and my creased and stained copy of *To Kill a Mockingbird* into my locker and made my way towards the office just as the shriek of the bell started up.

"Hey, where are you going?" Brigitte called out. I kept my head down, pretending I hadn't heard.

I couldn't deal with Brigitte now. She stood a moment, undecided, and then followed me.

"What's up, Lucy?" she said. "You look kinda funny."

I stopped in the shade of the walkway. I had no choice. "I feel a bit weird. I might have glandular fever."

"It's going 'round," said Brigitte, sympathetically.

Everyone had clattered into classrooms and it was hushed in that way the world gets immediately after a din. In a minute, a teacher would come past, shooing and flapping at the stragglers.

Brigitte had her puzzled, baffled look on and I remembered us as shy kindy girls. Her legs were far too long for her body, back then; they still were. I put my arm about her shoulder, my friend Briggy with whom I'd shared my first period cramps – naturally I thought I was dying back then, too. I hadn't had time for her lately and here she was being a good friend. Suddenly, I felt grateful to her for stopping, for caring.

"How are you? I heard you won your state final? The 200-metre swim? Amazing." Before Natasha had come into my life, I would have probably seen the race; at the very least held the stopwatch for her at the local pool when she was training.

Now, I felt guilty that I hadn't even rung her up to congratulate her. She said: "It was really nice of your mum to wish me luck before the competition."

That made me feel worse. Some friend I was. I had been so into Natasha that I had forgotten all about probably the most exciting event in my friend's life. I said: "How's Noah? Is Nev still being abusive to women?" Brigitte smiled. "Just the same."

"What about Winston?" Being owners of dogs with short legs and long bodies was another reason we had been friends for so long.

"And your mum and dad?" I realised I had missed them, too. When we were 10, I drove with them in their ancient Volvo to Noosa where we stayed in an apartment with shiny big tiles overlooking the beach. They called me Lucky Lucy because I won at checkers ten times straight and we plaited each other's hair and ate toasted cheese sandwiches with strawberry jam – Noah's ones had tomato sauce – on the balcony as the light fell. Her mum was thin and tidy with a straight bob and an important job in the state health department. Her dad was a distracted professional with a ridiculous collection of practical jokes that always backfired. He'd always look doleful and Brigitte would pat his hand in consolation and her mother would take another gulp of chardonnay. Brigitte said, slowly, "Dad's moved out."

We stopped and I looked at her, appalled. My hand reached out for hers. She took it gratefully. "I'm so, so sorry, Briggy." Her eyes filled with tears and mine did, too. "Is he coming back?" She shrugged. "Dunno."

"How's Noah doing?"

"Noah's being Noah."

Before I knew it, I'd offered to go over that afternoon.

"We could watch Netflix together." Brigitte sounded excited. That was just what I needed to do today. "You're on. Meet you at the back gate this afternoon."

She nodded and gave my hand a squeeze. Suddenly, I no longer felt sick. Perhaps I'd go to class, after all.

Hot afternoons always brought out the lead pencil smell of the classroom. Being late to class meant I was in the last row with the window behind me.

Across the aisle, Lindsay was working on a text. When no one was looking, she sent it to Emma, whose phone lit up and beeped. Staring straight ahead, she typed furiously. Lindsay was next. She read it, snorted and when no one was looking forwarded it on until, eventually, it hit my phone. I looked at the message: *who was getting it on in weights room?* My stomach began to churn up again with a terrible feeling of shame. With shaking hands, I turned off my phone and pushed it into my pencil case.

Except for Natasha, I hadn't told anyone about Paul and me kissing. How did it get out? Was he showing off by telling them we'd hooked up?

Straight after the bell, I went looking for Natasha. Of course, I couldn't find her. I asked just about every girl in our class.

"Hasn't she left already for the station with Lindsay and Emma?" said one girl, Kim.

"I thought she went home early," said Kim's friend, Georgia. "I hope you find her. You're lucky they even talk to you."

"I hear they sometimes come straight to school from their night out," said Kim.

Yeah, real lucky. I tried to grab a drink from the bubbler, but the water pressure was nil and the water just dribbled down the spout.

Best thing to do, I decided, was to head home. I'd send Natasha a message from there. Maybe she'll respond when we're not at school. I picked up my bag and hoisted it onto my back and began the trudge home. Halfway there I remembered Brigitte.

Brigitte. Oh, god. I had forgotten to meet her like I'd promised. I stood in the middle of the footpath and with trembling fingers sent her a text. I stared at the phone for a full five minutes, but there was no reply. I sent another, this one full of sad faces. Still nothing. I slowly returned the phone to my blazer pocket.

I found my mother inside the kitchen pantry. There was a paperback face-down on a box of toilet paper so I knew she'd been reading in there even though it was getting close to dinner time. I did that, too. Or I used to, sitting on the little stepladder with the door pulled to and reading chapter after chapter undisturbed.

She took one look at my face and swiped up the dog leads. "We're going to walk the dogs and talk about it."

Nothing helps like a dog who resembles party food. I was in.

It all came out. Okay, not the part about me being, basically, 'slut-shamed' but everything else, including what I'd done to Brigitte that afternoon.

"It sounds to me like you are not being a good friend to Brigitte and Natasha's not being a good friend to you. What are you going to do?"

I hate it when your mum throws it back to you. It requires taking a long hard look at yourself and then doing something that may be good for you but that makes you feel horribly uncomfortable while doing it.

"I have to say sorry to Brigitte and make it up to her."

"Right."

I immediately took out my phone and began to work up a text. Mum put out a hand to stop me.

"Brigitte deserves a face-to-face or, at the very least, a phone call. Not a text."

She was right. I rang as soon as we got home from the walk. Brigitte listened to me say sorry about 100 times without interruption.

"That's all right, Lucy," she said tonelessly when I'd finished. "I had to do stuff this afternoon anyway." Her mouth moved away from the phone to speak to her mother. "Sorry, have to go. Dad's coming over soon to pick up some things and Mum doesn't want to be here when he does." Her voice caught in her throat and she hung up. I blew out a sigh and went to find mum.

"How did it go?"

Mum was peeling potatoes for dinner, the skins landing in the compost bin. The landline rang. It was Mrs Rooney from the retirement home. She knew it wasn't her usual day to have dinner with us, but would we pick Gert up? She was upsetting the other residents.

"How?"

"Winning at bingo and lording it over the losers."

After dinner, we propped up Aunt Gert on a couple of cushions so she could digest her meal. She opened her carpet bag and burrowed around for a hanky. When it was found, she honked into it so fiercely she let out a fart.

"What are you smirking at?" Aunt Gert clutched her bag to her concave chest. "I've got excellent metabolism. At my age, it's a gift."

Milly giggled. Aunt Gert glared at her.

"Shouldn't you be in bed?"

"It's only 8 o'clock. How did bingo go today?"

"I won. Ha! That should wipe the smile off May Gilbert's face. She sure has tickets on herself."

"Don't you like Mrs Gilbert?" Milly said.

"Can't stand her. She's bossy and talks too much and her pearls are fakes."

Absently, I put my hand up to touch my pendant, forgetting for a second I didn't have it anymore. I hoped that Aunt Gert wouldn't notice it gone. She had surprisingly beady eyes for an old person with cataracts. Suddenly, I wished I hadn't given it to Natasha.

"Lucy, my girl come sit by me. Before your dad takes me back to prison, you can tell me why you look so glum. I bet I can help."

Since she once advised me against playing hockey because it would give me gateposts for legs, I didn't think so but I sat beside her, anyway.

"Is it about your love life? This'll be good, but you'll have to spill the beans fast, I can hear your dad coming for me. Who's the fella? I've got issues too. We can compare notes. Does your boyfriend have a pulse? Mine doesn't, so you're already ahead of the game. I'll bet your young man is a hottie." She nudged me again. "Am I right? I can tell by your smile that he is. Well, what the hell is the problem? You should see Mr Grace at breakfast with his napkin tucked into his shirt like a big baby and his hair sticking up all over the place. It's not pretty."

How do I tell Aunt Gert that my love life was one big mess. I was being set up with one guy, being felt up by another and was making eyes at a third, who didn't even know I existed.

Aunt Gert patted my hand. "You must live your life, Lucy my girl. But stay true to yourself. You're beautiful and clever and kind. Don't forget it. And you don't need boys to make you feel better. It's all here, inside." She pointed to my full stomach, but I think she was talking about my heart.

Dad stuck his head in the room, then the rest of his body.

"Time to go, Gert." He took one arm and I took the other and together we hauled her out of her seat.

"Thanks for a lovely dinner," said Aunt Gert, dangling between our arms. "Sure beats the heck out of the puree they serve up at the home." We loaded her into the car, pushed the giant carpet bag in after her and Dad took off with a piece of Aunt Gert's skirt flapping out of the door.

Mum and I walked back inside with our arms about each other. "It's scary to think that you're related to her by blood," said Mum. I laughed, but I didn't mind.

Chapter 15

After Gert had left, I lay across my bed with my feet resting against the wall and my phone under my pillow, reading *Rebecca* and freaking myself out. Rebecca was so rich and beautiful. Was she really as bad as the book made out? Making evil pretty was a sneaky thing to do.

I almost jumped out of my skin when the phone buzzed through my pillow.

"Guess what?"

It was Natasha, acting like nothing was wrong.

"What?" I was aiming for blasé but it came out sulky.

"Lindsay's parents are away this weekend and she's having a dinner party. We're all staying the night and we've decided to dress up for it. It's going to be amazing. I can't wait for Hugh to see me. What am I going to wear?"

"Umm, clothes?"

"Very funny. What's up with you?"

"Nothing. I'm just trying to figure out why you're telling me all this."

"Well, if you're going to be like that, I'll go. But first let me say that I've made Lindsay invite you, too."

She had? Did that mean Natasha had decided to put our friendship before boys? "Great. Okay. Well, thanks."

"No problem. See ya."

I hit 'end'.

I was relieved Natasha and I were still friends and she wasn't ignoring me. I must have misread the situation. There's no way she'd have spread that rumour about me and Paul. I was wrong about that too. Friends didn't do that to one another. And didn't Natasha just prove that she was still my friend by making Lindsay include me. My first dinner party. With boys and no parents.

No parents? OMG. Mine will never let me go. What should I do? With a slippery finger, I hit redial. "My mum can't find out that Lindsay's parents won't be there."

"Just say you're staying at my house," Natasha said.

When was the best time to deceive your parents? At bedtime when they'll be tired and confused? Or in the morning when they're distracted by the coffee machine and the million and one chores ahead of them? The thought of waiting all through the night was more than my nerves could take.

I found my mum in the kitchen, stacking the dishwasher. Dad was still out.

"There you are," said Mum, flicking the switch. "I was just about to look for you to tell you that the golf club rang to see if you could work on Saturday night?"

"I can't."

"Is it because of your fight with Brigitte?"

"No."

"You've got too much homework?"

"No. It's not that." I began to rearrange the fruit in the bowl.

"What then?" Mum pushed my hands away from squeezing bananas. "Don't do that. You'll bruise them."

"It's nothing, really. It's just that Natasha's asked me over on Saturday night."

I waited for Mum to say, "What a marvellous idea. You must go. And why don't you buy a new outfit to wear to it."

Instead, she told me that Ms Carlton had called her last Friday. Not again? I wondered if Sam's teachers were as diligent and prepared to work after hours like Ms Carlton …

"She's got some concerns."

My ears tuned in to the word, 'concerns'. What concerns?

"Mum? What did she want?"

"She has noticed that recently your marks haven't been up to their usual standard."

"I can explain that," I started to say.

Mum interrupted me. "It's not that."

"Well what is it? I mean, the HSC is still three years away. You don't want me burning out in Year 10, do you? Coz that could be child abuse."

"Stop it, Lucy. That's not funny. Ms Carlton is worried about you. She's wondering if you're still having trouble settling in. She's wondering if you'd like to make an appointment with the school counsellor. Talk about your feelings?"

See a psychologist and talk about my feelings? I must have looked as horrified as I felt.

"Very informally, just a chat, really," said Mum, back-pedalling.

I scrunched up a tea towel. The dinner party was slipping away.

"Well?" Mum watched my face carefully.

If I said yes to seeing the counsellor, would I be allowed to go to a dinner party and 'stay' at Natasha's on Saturday night? It was worth a shot.

"Maybe," I said cautiously testing the waters.

"Great. I'll call Ms Carlton on Monday."

"Ummm, okay." It was now or never. "Umm, Natasha rang before. There's this dinner party at Lindsay's on Saturday night and I've been invited.

And – get this – Natasha's invited me to stay at her place afterwards. I really want to go."

Mum let out a breath slowly, "We don't usually allow sleepovers over during term-time, but let's see. I'll talk it over with your dad."

Back in my room, I picked up my English assignment on *The Great Gatsby*. It wouldn't kill me to get a start on it. As much as I wanted to be a social success, I didn't want to fail at school. By the time Mum and Dad knocked on my door – they were sticklers for respecting privacy – I had answered two questions and was working on the third.

I looked up at them, surprised. I had almost forgotten about the dinner party and wanting to stay at Natasha's.

"You can go to the dinner party but we don't want you staying overnight. We'll pick you up at 11. How's that?"

"11 o'clock!" No one had such an early curfew. I nearly said so, but when I saw my mother's nostrils flare – a sign that her usual easy-going approach to life was dwindling fast – I wisely shut my trap. She always held on to her temper the longest in the family, but when she lost it, she *lost* it. I returned to listening to Dad. He was saying that while they expected me to concentrate on my school work, they also wanted me to have a good time.

"All work and no play makes people very dull and very stressed. But you have a gift, kiddo: a brain.

Don't waste it," he said. He sat down heavily on the corner of the bed. He took off his glasses to rub his eyes. His face looked bare without them. His hair was up in tufts. I loved those tufts – so mad scientist. Well, he was an out-of-work geologist. He was also an idealist. It was his position on climate change and his concern with the effects of mining on our environment that had led to his retrenchment. To be honest, I was very proud of him and I liked to think that I held with the same ideology. Glasses back on, he reached out an arm to bring me closer. I hugged him back. An 11 o'clock curfew was a bummer but at least I was going. Mum switched out the light as they left my room.

"Nighty night. I'll call Lindsay's mother tomorrow."

Damn. I hadn't thought of that. I didn't sleep a wink all night for worry about what Lindsay's mum would say to mine. By the morning, I had a plan. I would somehow convince my mum not to call. It left me, still, with two other problems. I had to find something awesome to wear. I also had to say 'no' to a sleepover with Natasha. I hoped she wouldn't be too disappointed.

Chapter 16

Friday morning. I waited at my locker for Natasha to finish brushing her hair. By the time, she had switched to gloss application I was jiggling on the spot.

"What's up, Lucy? It's like you've got ADHD."

"Very funny. It's just that don't have anything to wear to Lindsay's."

"I've got one word for you. Westfield."

How could I tell her I didn't have enough money to go shopping at Westfield? She pouted in the little travel mirror she'd pinned to her locker door. "I'll take you this afternoon."

I knew I had debating practice after school. "Sure," I said.

That afternoon as soon as we left the school gates, we tied our jumpers around our waists and shoved our hats in our bags. We released our ponytails, stretching the band over our wrists and shaking our hair out in the toilets on Platform One. Strolling out from the waiting room afterwards, I noticed two guys from Northcote Grammar keeping tabs on us. Natasha totally ignored them, but it gave me a buzz. I wanted to nudge her and say: "Don't you have any idea. Being checked out is better than … finishing all your weekend homework on Friday night." But I didn't. I wasn't *that* stupid.

The top ten hits were on high rotation at Sportsgirl. We both sang along as we dumped our bags at the entrance and went inside. She sauntered over to a rack of crop tops. I ran my fingers along the racks of lacy hair bands and beads. When would be the best time to tell Natasha I couldn't stay over on Saturday night? *Never.* Come on! How bad could it be? It's not like I'm never going to stay there again. I picked up a belt. A sales girl wearing a belted tunic over skinny jeans and combat boots appeared beside me. The name on her colourful striped badge was Nicky.

"These belts are *sooo* great. I'm wearing one. Look. You wrap them around your waist twice, like this. See?" I looked at her tiny waist and indeed I saw. She blew a bubble, pop, and continued in a sing-song voice.

"Get me if you wanna try anything on." She bounced over to a mother shopping with her self-conscious pre-teen, a squirt with braces. I peered over the racks for Natasha and found her at a tub of rubber bracelets. Several items of clothing dangled from her fingers.

"Hey. What do you think of this?" I held up the belt.

"Nice," she said, nodding in time to the music.

"I'm going to try on these." She held up a floral cut-away shirt and some other floaty things. "Come with me."

We took numbered cards from another attractive Sportsgirl assistant. (Were symmetrical facial features a requisite of working there?) The change room was open-plan. Damn. There was nothing worse than exposing your non-Victoria's Secret underwear in public. Natasha was totally unconcerned. Well, I would be, too, if I had a body like hers. She didn't even bother to go into a corner. In the middle of the change room floor, in front of about ten other women including me, she dropped her uniform to the ground and went to work in front of a mirrored wall.

"What do you think?" Natasha examined herself critically in the floral cut-away shirt over a straight skirt. She liked what she saw, because she threw her weight onto one foot and dipped her hip into a runway pose. A glimpse of tanned stomach peeked out from between the skirt and shirt.

I put on white dungarees; one like the mannequin in the window had been wearing, and wrapped the pink belt around, twice. Bad look. I took it off and tried on jeans and an off-the-shoulder top. Better. I contorted to see if I could make out the price on the tag. The jeans were $99.95; the top was $59.95. Mum would have a fit. I sighed. Maybe just the belt, then. I turned to face Natasha. She was back in her uniform.

"Did you buy them?" I asked her.

"Yup. You?"

"I'm thinking about it." I dangled the belt away from me, looking at it and pretending to consider the belt.

"You like?"

"Sure. But I won't get it today. Might bring my mum back later. I'll see." I chewed at my lip. I didn't want Natasha to know that my mum probably wouldn't buy it for me.

"Okay. Well, let's get out of here".

"Just give me a sec." I found my uniform and put it on. I left my castoffs in a giant box just outside the changing room.

On the way out, I paused at a tub of bags.

"Move it, Lucy." Natasha pushed me towards the exit. I resisted. "What's with the rush?"

"Let's just *go.*"

Natasha was already through the door and picking up our bags. She handed me mine and we slung them over our shoulders. I turned back to say good-bye to the sales girl. She'd been nice. Natasha gave me another shove, harder this time. I stumbled. "Hey. What was that for? I was just being polite."

But Natasha was already half-way up the mall. I hurried after her.

"Is anyone behind us?" She said puffing slightly. I looked back.

"No. Why?"

"Tell you later. Keep on walking."

At the top of the mall, she stopped.

"Come in here," and she dragged me into the foyer of a building. She looked around. No one was in sight. She lifted her dress. I gasped. Underneath I could see a grey belt with silver studs.

"No way. Did you, like, steal it?" I was horrified. She rolled her eyes – I was such a princess – and lowered her dress.

"Yes way. It was easy."

"What about the tag?"

"Didn't have one."

"You can't do that. What if you get caught?"

"What if *we* get caught, you mean?" She gave me a sly grin. I gasped again. I didn't want to get caught stealing – god – especially on top of two Bs for English.

"You mean …" All of a sudden, I felt faint and dropped my head between my knees the way they taught you in first aid class. The air pressure changed as a heavy glass office door opened.

"We gotta get out of here," she said. "Pull it together, would you."

We fell out of the foyer onto the mall where nothing had changed. The sun was still shining and people were still moving up and down, yapping and going about their business at a hundred miles an hour. I pulled my head down tortoise-style, half expecting the shout of an angry security guard from down the hill. We hurried along the mall until we got to The Lemon Tree coffee shop.

Natasha flung down her bag and, pointing her finger, said with a smirk, "You should see your face."

"I can't believe you just did that," I said collapsing at a Formica table.

"We, Lucy. You were with me, don't forget. What? Don't look at me like that. I'm just saying. Anyway, the belt's for you." She leaned over and opened up her bag. "And these." She tugged something from her bag but didn't show me straightaway. "Close your eyes and give me your arm." And she threaded something onto my outstretched arm. "Open up." She leaned back in the tub chair to see my reaction.

"You have to admit it, I'm good," she said with a satisfied smile. I smiled back, I couldn't help it. There we were, sitting grinning at each other, dizzy from the high of doing something illegal and getting away with it. Natasha, the golden girl, and me, boring old Lucy Johnson, who now, by association, was as cool as ice cream. I felt a small thrill run through me like a sparkler. I bent over and folded down my socks so that they were really short. There, gotta look the part. Natasha twisted to catch a waitress.

"Two cappuccinos, please, with extra chocolate on top." When they arrived, she clinked her mug to mine.

"Here's to Saturday night." We stared at one another. Then I told her.

Her blue eyes grew hard, but she tossed her head as if she didn't care a fig.

"Don't worry about it. It's cool. You can't help it if you've got controlling parents who still treat you like a baby."

We caught the train home pretty much in silence. Natasha had unwound the belt and shoved it into my bag. The bracelets were burning a hole in my skin. I fiddled with them in misery and stared at the trees rushing past, while Natasha texted other more interesting people on her phone. Mine was the first stop and I stepped off slowly, turning at the last minute.

"See you tomorrow. Thanks for the stuff."

"See ya," she said without looking up.

Chapter 17

I'd let Natasha down and still didn't have anything to wear by the time I woke up on Saturday morning. Perhaps it would be best if I didn't go. It would solve the problem of Mum ringing Lindsay's mum and finding out that she wasn't even there.

"Feel my glands. They're up and I feel kinda sick, like I have a temperature. I've got a headache and I might vomit. I don't think I can go out tonight."

Mum pushed her spectacles on the top of her head but didn't glance up from sewing my sister's name in a frog suit made of a slime green leotard, green tights and garden gloves the colour of toxic waste for her upcoming ballet concert. "Well, if you're sure."

That was easy. Then Mum started up with the psychological stuff.

"Do you think your symptoms might be nerves. It's your first dinner party. It's understandable that you'd be anxious. Anyone would be. Sometimes, it's better to feel your fear and do it anyway. You'll be fine. Just be yourself."

I couldn't tell her that being myself was exactly what I was afraid of.

I wandered into my room and flopped on the bed. After a while, I got up and went to my wardrobe. I found myself pulling out skirts, tops and jeans and putting them together in different ways. One outfit – shorts and a top – looked kinda okay. I'd pack a pair of jeans, just in case I got cold. I flung the rubber bracelets across the bed so that they resembled a Venn diagram.

My phone rang. It was Natasha.

"Lindsay wants us over there early. She's having a crisis. How soon can you get here?"

"Your headache's gone, then?" said my mother dryly when I asked if she could drop me off early.

Lindsay wrenched open her door and stood there, her fringe all teased up as if she'd been dragged around by her hair. She was fuming.

"Where the hell have you all been? I've been going mad here."

"Don't freak, Linds. We're here," said Natasha, and we traipsed past her into the lounge room.

Natasha flung down her Country Road canvas bag jammed with her stuff and made herself at home, ready to play grown-ups in a room of white-slipped sofas, floral papered walls and wicker baskets that had been arranged artfully in a corner at the suggestion of a decorator. We all sat down on Lindsay's white sofa.

"Shame Emma couldn't be here," said Lindsay.

"To be honest, I'm a bit sick of Emma," said Natasha.

We spent about three hours pottering around the house, unpacking our outfits, fiddling with our hair and scrolling through recipes on our phones. We were like wives waiting for their husbands to come home.

"What're we having for dinner?" Natasha asked from the bathroom where she was rubbing a finger in a pot of Lindsay's mum's moisturiser. Lindsay had no idea. She'd been so busy with her hair that she'd forgotten all about the food.

"Let's Google it."

"What do you think of this one?" said Lindsay, holding out her phone.

"Chicken curry? Perfect," said Natasha.

"What do we need?" I peered at the list of ingredients. "Chicken breast, a tin of coconut cream, onion, rice."

"We don't have any of that," said Lindsay.

"What about beef ragu? Guys really like red meat. My mum used to make it all the time; she said it was easier than it looked," said Natasha.

Lindsay read out the instructions.

"I don't know. It sounds pretty hard to me," I said doubtfully.

"And we need fillet of beef, whatever that is," said Lindsay. "Mum left a couple of steaks in the fridge. Would they do?"

Natasha said: "Dunno, Linds."

"What about pasta? Mum's got some of that in the pantry," said Lindsay.

"Here's a tomato sauce that this website says is foolproof." Natasha read out the ingredients.

"Perfect." Lindsay celebrated by opening a packet of gummy bears.

The menu sorted, we turned to more important matters: our bodies. With no parents to hassle us, we painted our toenails in the lounge room on the glass coffee table, scattering cotton wool all over the carpet.

"God, Lucy. Are you for real?"

"What do you mean?" I looked across at Lindsay.

"Those. What are those?" She was pointing to my hairy legs. Natasha laughed.

I crossed my legs. I hadn't shaved in a while. Big deal. I'd change into jeans.

"Haven't you ever heard of a Brazilian?" said Natasha.

"What's a Brazilian?"

"It's a waxing procedure that removes all the hair on your vagina."

"No way!" I shuddered. I'd rather be buried alive than have all the hair ripped from me like that.

"A bikini wax will be enough. Lindsay, have you got any wax?" Lindsay fetched an old tub of wax from the chemist that she overheated in the microwave. It hurt like hell and left red burn marks. As I blew on my inner thigh and contemplated my third-degree burns, Lindsay said, "You're next, Natasha."

"Not without something to numb the pain," she said, firmly. "What have you got?"

Lindsay opened her dad's liquor cabinet and surveyed the assortment of funny shaped bottles.

"Advocaat, whatever that is, it's bright yellow like snot, so probably not. What about Gordon's gin? We've also got sherry. I think my granny drinks that. Or there's tawny port. Basically, we've got the lot. What do you want?"

"Where's the vodka?"

"Dunno," Lindsay said. "Freezer, I think."

"Can't use that then," said Natasha.

"Why not?" I was curious.

"Because if we put in water to hide the fact that we've been drinking, the vodka will freeze and give the game away for Linds. We'd better stick with the gin."

Lindsay collected several glasses from the kitchen and cranked up the record player. We were going to have a party before the party.

"I'm hungry. Got anything to eat?" I said, eventually.

"There are chips in the kitchen," said Lindsay, twisting the lid of an old bottle of port.

Tearing open packets of salt and vinegar chips and pouring them into bowls seemed hysterically funny especially when they fell all over the floor.

At about 7, Natasha disappeared into the bathroom and didn't come out for ages. When she did she looked amazing in a fitted floral midriff top and short straight skirt.

Lindsay gave her an evil look. "What have you been doing in there? I've been in the kitchen, like, forever."

"God, Lindsay. Relax, would you," said Natasha. Her eyes glittered brightly, too brightly. "Dinner parties aren't rocket science, you know. The guys won't even notice what they're eating."

"Then why are we even bothering?" Lindsay flounced over to the sofa on heels a size too big and threw herself onto it, just as the doorbell rang. "Get it, would you? I'm sick of this."

Natasha yanked open the door.

"Hugh," she squealed and fell into his arms.

Hugh and Sam both stared at her. She was acting pretty drunk.

I stood back, sober and nervous. I had tipped most of my drinks into one of Lindsay's mum's potted orchids when no one was looking and I was conscious of my stinging thighs.

"Come in, sit down, make yourselves at home." Natasha ushered them to the sofa, sending Sam in first beside Lindsay, then me. She put Hugh on the opposite sofa and slid in beside him.

"Let me get you a drink?" she waved her arms towards the drinks cabinet. "Pick your poison."

"Surprise us," Hugh said. When she'd poured two glasses to the brim with something brown she said, "Who likes Lucy's bracelets?" and ran the tips of her fingers down them.

"Very pretty," said Hugh, but his eyes were on Natasha. I didn't mind. I tried to think of something clever to say, came up with nothing and instead shook them.

"Ask her where she got them?" Natasha nuzzled him and swung her crossed legs to show him her shoes as well as her black G string. "You smell gorgeous. How was cricket today?"

"Hot," said Hugh. He said nothing more.

"Now you're supposed to ask her a question about her day," I said helpfully across Natasha to Hugh.

For the first time, he looked at me. "Huh?"

"Well, to have a conversation we have to exchange information. You know, like, I say what's your favourite colour? You say blue. What's yours? And I say, green. So on. It's really easy."

"Teal. My favourite colour is teal."

"As in bluey-greeny-grey?"

"Yup."

"That's an unusual colour for a guy."

Hugh's eyes crinkled into a very attractive smile, but this time he was looking at me not Natasha. "I'm an unusual guy," he said. Sam snorted, too loudly, at that.

"Can you get me a drink?" Natasha brought Hugh's focus back to her with her slender arm, pointing and waving. "Drinks cabinet is over there."

"Sure," said Hugh. "But haven't you had enough?"

"What are you? My father?"

I swiped up a handful of peanuts and tossed them into my mouth, but I was nervous, I guess. I began to choke and Sam had to thump me on the back. "Cough them up. Or I'll have to perform the Heimlich on you."

"Or mouth-to-mouth," hooted Natasha.

"I'm fine." I took a gulp from the nearest drink. Straight vermouth. I gagged. "Bathroom, excuse me."

The doorbell chimed as I escaped down the hall to the bathroom, leaning against the wall to steady myself, a hand on the towel rack. The salmon pink towels were still damp from our showers. The bathroom looked a wreck. There was make-up all over the vanity and clothes strewn on the floor. I drank straight from the tap, wiped my hand against the damp towel and closed the bathroom door behind me.

One more guest had arrived in my absence. I saw him as soon as I returned to the living room and it brought up my bile when he winked at me. I backed up, and escaped towards the kitchen.

Natasha stood up. She swayed a little, regained her balance and, with a finger pointing forwards, headed in my direction. "I'll come, too." She stopped, swayed some more, and returned to give Hugh a big kiss.

"Try not to miss me while I'm gone."

I fumed in the kitchen. "Who invited him?"

"Not me," said Natasha.

"Who then?"

Natasha shrugged.

I began to pace. "I've got to go. I can't stay."

"Don't you dare leave me with Lindsay." Natasha hissed under her breath.

Just then, Lindsay flew in to the kitchen. "Don't just stand there," she put on her mother's apron and picked up a wooden spoon and began to stir the hell out of a saucepan of tomato sauce. "Help me."

"How exactly?" I said, wringing my hands. I still couldn't believe that Paul was here, in the next room.

"Fuck knows." She dropped the spoon in the sauce to examine her phone on the counter, "Shit. Shit. Shit. What's next?"

"Stay calm, Linds." Natasha pushed the spoon handle in my direction. "Stir this," she ordered. Yes. Good. Cooking would be a distraction. I stirred. "What's after this?"

"Do I look like I have a clue?" Lindsay dropped her phone and took another swallow of her pink drink. She gave it to Natasha and turned on the tap to fill yet another saucepan. It sprayed all over her and covered the floor. She sprang back and slipped in her heels in the water and went down, hard on her butt. I pulled her up noticing that tears had sprung up.

"Stir, Lucy. Natasha, stop taking my drink. There's a knife over there. Cut up the salad."

I didn't know much about cooking but I was pretty sure that lettuce was meant to be gently torn rather than chopped. Natasha began cutting.

I turned off the sauce. "That's ready. What do you want me to do now?"

But Lindsay had no idea. She poured another drink.

"I know. I'll cook the pasta." I shook the pasta from the packet into the water. It fizzed over.

"Hey, what's going on in there? We're getting hungry," called out Sam.

Lindsay nearly went ballistic. Natasha and I calmed her down. "Easy does it. We can do this," I said. We were united by a common cause: feeding the guests.

When we eventually got the sauce onto the pasta and into bowls and on the table, dinner looked like a dog's breakfast.

"Don't even speak," said Lindsay through gritted teeth as she banged a bowl down in front of Hugh.

Chapter 18

"Here's what I'm wondering …" Paul reared back in his chair, chest out, legs wide. "If you were stranded on a desert island, but you were allowed to have three things, what would they be?"

Dinner was over and, while the leftovers congealed on plates, we played a game.

Natasha laughed. "That's easy: hair dryer, moisturiser and eyelash curler." She picked up a Tim Tam, her second.

Sam said, "You'd die of dehydration and hunger but you'd leave a beautiful corpse. Is that it?"

"What would you take?" Natasha began to crumble the biscuit in her fingers.

"Hammock, fishing rod and Red Bull," said Sam promptly. "I'm a survivalist."

"What about you, Lindsay?" Paul leaned across to pour more wine into her glass. Some sloshed onto the table. She squinted at him from under her lashes.

"Why is everybody looking at me?"

"We're waiting for your answer."

"To what?" She leaned over as if to take a nap, her eyelids drooping.

"What three things you'd take to a desert island?"

"Oh. I'd take my friends. Definitely. Natasha and Emma," She lifted her head and slipped sideways onto Paul's shoulder. "I might take you, too". She kissed him.

I stood up quickly to clear up and reached for the nearest plate.

When I returned from my first load, the room had emptied. I blinked at Hugh's jacket still swinging on the back of a chair.

"Where'd everyone go?"

Sam stood in the doorway with a handful of plates. "Where do ya think?" My cheeks burned.

"Where do you want these plates?"

"Where-ever." I waved my hand in the general direction of the sink already piled high.

"I think I want to just sit down."

"Oh, okay."

We sat down on one of the sofas. We were alone. I put several cushions between us. I hoped he didn't notice.

"Great dinner."

I grimaced. "Do you think?"

"Oh, yeah. Absolutely."

"It's surprisingly hard to get everything ready at the same time."

"I'd believe it."

"What's the time?"

"10. Why?"

"My mum's picking me up at 11."

"Not staying the night?"

"Nope. Are you?"

"Nope."

"Is Hugh?"

"No idea."

"Isn't he your brother?

"Yep."

"And you don't know?"

"That's the way we roll in our family."

"Is he your only brother?"

"Thank god."

"I feel the same way about my sister. We were home schooled last few years. Nearly drove me crazy?"

"Home schooled? How come?"

"We had to live out of town, close to my dad's work. He worked for a mining company."

"Wow. What was it like, being home schooled?"

"All right, I guess."

"Was it hard?"

"Not really. Mum's a teacher and she let me work at my own pace. Mostly, I was ahead. Maybe it's why I got the scholarship."

"Was it lonely?"

"Sometimes. But I could Skype my old friends and stuff. Once a week, we'd go into the local school so we could 'socialise' and spend a day in the classroom. That was okay. Sometimes it was easier to stay home. I have cute dogs. Sid and Nancy. It was cool to hang with them every day."

"Better than a brother, I reckon."

"Have you got any pets?"

"Not since we moved. We've had some pretty weird pets. Hugh once had a snake. We called it Kaa. I know, I know, a bit of a cliché. Anyway, one day it escaped. We couldn't find it for days. Guess who found it? The president of one of Mum's medical committees. They were over at our house having a meeting or whatever and she sat down on one of our fancy armchairs. Mum said she shot up so fast when the pillow underneath her started to move. And there it was – Hugh's snake, relaxing inside the cushion. Hilarious. Anyway, Hugh got into heaps of trouble and he had to give old Kaa to the science department at school. He's still there in one of the science classrooms. I visit him sometimes. The science master lets me hold him but only if I wear goggles. Kaa's developed a bad habit of going for people's eyes."

"He might be lonely. Do snakes get lonely?"

"Dunno. Maybe," said Sam, thinking about it.

"You and Hugh get on pretty okay now?"

Sam shrugged. "I guess. We don't fight so much anymore, if that's what you mean. But I wouldn't want to home-school with him."

"You used to fight?"

"We nearly killed each other as kids. See that scar?" He held up his hand, palm facing me, "That hole there? That's from when Hugh stabbed me with a pocket knife when we were about 10 years old. I had to have five stitches."

I sympathised. "I guess it's hard when you are so close in age. There's nearly five years between me and my sister so no competition. I sometimes have to babysit her but that's okay. I don't mind. She can be annoying, but she's sometimes okay. Don't tell her I said that."

"As far as my parents are concerned, Hugh is the golden boy. They are always comparing us. I hate that. It's like that at school, too. Hugh's in the A's in cricket and rowing. He's a sergeant in cadets and stuff like that. As soon as my teachers work out that they've got Hugh's brother in the class, they say some smart-arsed thing like 'you've got big shoes to fill.' Some of them taught my father, which is even worse."

"What do you do?"

"I get into trouble just to show them that they can't compare us."

I wrapped my arms around my knees. "I get it."

"One time I wagged school. I'd had enough."

"Where did you go? The oval? The beach?"

"Nah. I just rode around on the train, reading *The Fellowship of the Ring*. Best day of my life."

I laughed.

"Yeah, what a rebel," he said, wryly.

"You're funnier than Hugh. You can't play tennis, though."

"Thanks for that," he said.

"Any time." I played with the piping around the cushion between us.

"I know what it's like to feel invisible. Everyone always notices Natasha and never me."

"I don't know about that," said Sam, not quite meeting my eyes. I worried, then, that he thought I was fishing for compliments. I changed subjects, "Let's play a game."

He groaned, "Not Truth or Dare again."

"God, no." I saw that there were cards in a wicker basket on the sideboard. I went over and got them. "Let's play Snap."

"Okay. I'm pretty good at this game. I have to warn you about that."

"So am I."

Sam lowered himself to the floor, sitting cross-legged and putting his back against the sofa. His elbows rested against his knees. I flopped on the floor opposite and rearranged myself so that I was lying flat on my stomach with my legs stretched out like Milly's.

Our elbows kept slipping and our hands stung as they slapped the cards. Whenever I looked across at him, he was looking at me. I noticed that in the dim light his eyes appeared more grey than green. I lowered my eyes, feeling shy. I saw the time on his watch. Shit. It was nearly 11. I leapt to my feet.

"Mum's going to be here soon. I'd better go outside."

"I'll wait with you," said Sam.

"Okay."

Sam gathered the cards and stood up. I could feel the heat of Sam's body through the dark. Then he sort of bear hugged me, folding me up in his arms and squeezing. He smelled like warm biscuits.

"Mmmmm …" I mumbled into his chest.

"What was that?" he said. I drew back. Did I just mmmm out loud?

"Nothing. I need to go to the bathroom."

I trotted down hall, feeling better. I ignored the closed bedroom doors to my left and right. I wasn't about to imagine what was happening on the other side of them. The bathroom door was ajar. I pushed it wider, stepped inside, then froze. Too late, Paul had seen me. He finished urinating and, slowly, with a sly smile, zipped himself up.

"Like what you see?

When Sam found me, I was sitting in the gutter, looking up and down the street, my arms across my knees.

"There you are." He stood above me. "What's up?"

I shook my head. "Nothing."

I heard the sound of an approaching car. "That's my mum." I stood up. "Say good bye to Natasha for me."

"Sure."

He looked so nice standing there. Before I knew it, I had leaned over and kissed his cheek. "Thanks for waiting with me."

"No problem," he said. "Um, have you heard about the debating team pairing up?" he looked at me a bit anxiously, "We're together."

"I know," I said, getting up.

Chapter 19

He loves me, he loves me not.

It was a silly game Milly used to play. But there I was, heading to the station on Monday morning, plucking petals. Pluck, pluck, pluck.

He loves me not.

That settled it. Sam and I would just be friends. That was okay. Sam and I had a lot in common. But I didn't feel the same way about him as I did about Nick. Nick Hall was gorgeous and every time I saw him, my heart beat 100 times faster. My heart didn't do anything unusual around Sam. Sure, Nick had a girlfriend. So what? It wasn't like they were married or anything. Nick Hall was perfect for me. It was obvious. Natasha would totally approve when we got together.

I checked my phone. No messages. But, whoa, look at the time. I'd better step on it or I'd be late for the train. Or, rather, too late to hang out on the station.

They were all there, huddled in the waiting room that stank of mice and trashy celebrity fragrance, passing around a packet of low fat Piranhas and rating the bystanders. Natasha was there, of course, along with Emma and Lindsay and two other girls, Kate and Sophie, who I didn't really know. They parted to make room for me. I threw my bag down and looked around at the expectant faces with their shiny pale hair and lips.

"What are you talking about?" I said, looking around happily. This sense of belonging was the best feeling in the whole world.

"Last Saturday night." Natasha said.

"I wish I had been there instead of at my grandparents' boring ruby wedding anniversary," Emma pouted. Natasha was right: Emma could be annoying sometimes. The other girls began to fire questions.

"Did everyone look good?"

"What was Lindsay's dinner like?"

"What about you and Sam?"

"What did you wear?"

"Okay, what did I wear? Well, I wore jeans and a top that I pulled together with a belt and some bracelets that Natasha got me."

I felt in my element. "But you should have seen Natasha. She looked gorgeous. Hugh couldn't take his eyes off her."

I glanced sidelong at the girl who'd been so cold and unwelcoming when I'd first started at school. "Lindsay looked really good, too." Lindsay looked grateful. How quickly the pecking order changed.

"You should have seen the kitchen afterwards. Completely wrecked."

Kate swung around to Lindsay, "What did your parents say when they saw the mess?"

"They literally killed me. I am not kidding. I'm grounded for a month."

There was a sharp intake of breath around me.

"What is it?" I said. "What's wrong?"

"The Northcote Grammar Year 11 dinner dance is in two weeks," explained Kate. "Natasha and Lindsay are supposed to be going."

I felt myself grow cold. It was the first I'd heard of any dinner dance. How come Natasha had never mentioned it?

"Remember Reece's party last year? It was awesome."

"Isn't Reece the guy who last week hitched his skateboard to a truck all the way into town?" Emma took a bite of a green apple, her breakfast.

"People still talk about that party. It went viral."

"We should have a party like that," said Natasha.

"Maybe the dinner dance'll be like that?" I said.

"I'm going to that dinner dance if I have to commit murder to get there," said Lindsay.

Emma patted Lindsay's shoulder. "If it's any consolation, I'm not going either."

"Did you hear Amanda in double maths yesterday? She is so annoying."

"Not half as annoying as my mother," moaned Lindsay. "It's so unfair."

Natasha held up her hand. "Can we not talk about this for just a second? Sorry, Linds, but it's getting boring."

"Fine," said Lindsay and subsided, hurt.

"What I want to know is who does she think she is?" Natasha looked around. "Is anyone else kind of surprised at the way Amanda's bragging?"

"I guess," ventured Emma.

"What exactly did she say?" I had been in the double maths period but had been doing an extra problem in the back of my book when everyone else was allowed five minutes to recalibrate and Amanda had smugly started going on about how her boyfriend, Patrick, had booked a limousine to pick her up.

"It's soooo romantic." Emma imitated Amanda's high-pitched voice.

"I felt like putting my fingers down my throat. It's not like it's the formal or anything. They'd only be in it for about 10 seconds," declared Natasha. Amanda, apparently, only lived about ten feet from the golf club where the dinner dance was being held.

"What would that cost a second? Twenty bucks?" She was cross that Amanda was stealing her limelight.

"Don't worry," said Emma. "You and Hugh will be the best-looking couple there." She took another bite of her apple. "God, I'd better be losing weight. Do you think I have?"

We alighted and walked two by two down to school. Natasha and I walked together.

"Did you hear that Nick Hall broke up with his girlfriend? No? It was last Saturday night, at the oval. She tried to slit her wrists afterwards and had to go to hospital in an ambulance. You didn't hear about it? Well, you wouldn't. It wasn't a real suicide attempt. She was just trying to get attention. Well, I organised for Nick to take Lindsay to the dinner dance, as a favour to Hugh. We were going to double-date, you know?" I didn't know, had never been on a double-date, but that wasn't really the point and so I kept nodding and listening.

"Well, you know how Lindsay's grounded? She was planning to sneak out for this dinner. But Nick doesn't care. He told Hugh he wanted to go with someone else. So, who do you think Nick's going to ask?"

Should I attempt to answer or was it a rhetorical question? But I didn't have a clue.

"It's you."

"Me?" We had arrived at school. I stopped to stare at her.

"That's what Hugh says," said Natasha. She let the others go ahead before continuing, "He met you apparently and liked you. I don't remember you telling me you'd met." She yawned like it was no big deal. "Do you realise we're going to the dance with two of the hottest guys in Year 11."

I tried to smile. Lindsay and I were finally beginning to get along.

"You don't look very excited."

"Sorry. It's just that Lindsay's going to hate me for this."

"It's not your fault she's grounded."

"It kind of is," I said.

She stared at me. "You do want to go, don't you?"

I nodded. I really, really wanted to go. I wanted to dress up and look beautiful beside Nick Hall.

"Good. Nick's cute." As far as she was concerned it was all settled. I was going to the Northcote Grammar Year 11 dinner dance. She stretched out her neck. "I gotta go to class."

I was thrilled, I couldn't deny it, but I was petrified, too. Lindsay was going to totally freak if she found out that I was going instead of her.

"Hey, wait a sec."

"What is it?" She sounded a bit impatient.

"We have to keep from Lindsay that I am going

instead of her." To anyone else, it would have seemed an impossible task – betrayal, even. Not to Natasha. "Fine," she said, easily. "What are friends for?"

Chapter 20

This was *it*. My dream has come true. I couldn't wish for anything more. I was part of the A crowd. I was going to a boys' school dinner dance. My best friend was the most popular girl in the school. She wore her socks turned down twice, so did I. She lent me her lip gloss and daily after recess and lunch we'd reapply two coats over the shelf in the toilet block, ignoring the younger girls and those in our year whom Natasha deemed 'losers', as they jostled past. One time I passed Brigitte on her way to swimming squad. She pretended she didn't see me which saved me from having to cut short a conversation. But I didn't care. Not then, anyway. A sneery voice in my head said otherwise. Remember what you're doing to Lindsay, it said. I tried not to listen to it. I mostly succeeded.

And then Lindsay found out that Nick was taking someone else to the dinner dance.

It happened the following morning and the fallout could be heard as far away as the science lab. It was period two and Natasha and I were putting on our regulation blue ugly racerback Speedos in the changing room behind the pool with a bunch of other girls who couldn't come up with a good enough reason not to swim. There are only so many weeks in the month in which a girl can have her period.

The door slammed open and in she came, shrieking like a banshee. Natasha and I exchanged a quick look: we'd been waiting for this moment. So, we spent an extra second composing ourselves before we turned around. I had to look particularly innocent, a tough assignment considering how quickly my face dissolved under pressure. I braced myself for the performance of my life.

"Have you heard?" screeched Lindsay.

Natasha picked up Lindsay's hand and said ever so gently, "I know. Nick's taking someone else. But you were grounded. What else could he do?" She was the voice of reason.

Lindsay sank down, after the first shock had subsided, her eyes bulbous and vacant. When she spoke, her voice was toneless: "But I've already got the killer dress."

I tried not to look but was mesmerised by a fat slippery tear that skidded down to Lindsay's round chin and hung suspended for a second before smashing to the grey tiled floor.

"Lucy, could you give us a sec," said Natasha.

"Sure." I dropped my tunic on top of my shoes on the adjacent bench and backed out of there, hitting the corner of the bench with the edge of my knee as I went. The last thing I saw was the anguish on Lindsay's face as she listened to Natasha's whispers.

Whatever soothing words Natasha murmured worked because by the time we had assembled behind the courts at lunchtime, Lindsay was calm as she announced to everyone that because she was still grounded she wouldn't be attending the dinner dance. "I didn't really want to go anyway," she said, a note of defiance creeping in.

Everything went back to normal except that after school I walked alongside Natasha up to the station with Lindsay and Emma in the row behind.

"What happens now?" I asked, not really sure of the procedure.

"Nothing. We tell Nick."

I thought Nick already knew.

"Now? With Lindsay?"

Right before we got there, Natasha turned and spoke in a low voice to Lindsay and Emma, who both nodded and left us to stand at the other end of the platform.

"What did you say to them?"

"I told Emma to keep Lindsay away from Nick until she felt better," Natasha said, "Look, there they are."

The two boys were sprawled on the bench under the window outside the waiting room, but they both got up when we arrived. Natasha walked straight up to Hugh and kissed him with her eyes closed. The two of them broke apart and, smiling, Natasha took him by the hand and led him into the waiting room, leaving Nick and me standing there. This is so awkward, I thought, eyeing my feet. Should I say something or get my phone out and pretend I wasn't waiting for him to ask me out? I glanced up and there he was with his back against the door jamb, shit, just staring at me.

Bing. A text.

I fumbled around in my pocket for my phone. It was Natasha.

Say something.

I opened my mouth to speak but before any words could come out, Nick spoke.

"Hey, Lucy. How's Sid?"

"He's good," thinking, wow. He remembered.

"Natasha tells me you're coming to the dinner dance. That's cool." And that was that.

Later, in the vestibule of the train, our bags between our legs and our eyes half on the boys, mucking around on the step to the downstairs carriage, Natasha asked if I liked Nick.

Yes! I wanted to shout. I love him. "Course not," I said. "I hardly know him."

"That's good. He's on the rebound, you know, and I'd hate for you to get hurt."

"Don't worry, I won't."

"Hey, you'll get ready at mine, right?" said Natasha.

"Absolutely."

I was so relieved that I almost missed the platform when I stepped off the train and had to use my arms as windmills to get my balance.

"Hey, you forgot your bag." Natasha threw it out through the closing door. It hit the platform, hard, and sprang open releasing all my notes and folders all over the place.

"Oops, sorry." Natasha was just a white hand, fingers waggling at the window as the train pulled out.

"Doesn't matter," I said. But I felt like a complete idiot, running up and down the platform gathering up my books and folders and shoving them back into my bag. The slipstream had pulled some of my sheets of foolscap some way down the platform. I followed the trail. I found my dinner dance To Do list underneath a pensioner's orthotic shoe. She stumbled when I grabbed for it, screeching, "What do you think you're doing? Scaring old ladies?" She shook her stick at me, muttering, "The youth of today: drug pushers, the lot of you."

Chapter 21

I was calm by the time I got home. I took the key out of my pocket, unlocked the door and went inside. Someone leapt out at me from behind the front door. It gave me such a fright I dropped my key and screamed.

"Mum?" I said when I realised who it was. "What were you trying to do? Wait," I looked around for a hidden camera, "are we on *Prank Patrol?*"

"No. Way more exciting than that. Ms Carlton called."

I groaned. Not again.

"No, that's not the exciting part. She wanted to tell you that she's organised for a boy called Sam Curtis to come over tomorrow afternoon after school to work on your debate."

I looked at her in horror. "What? You're kidding."

"I thought you'd be pleased. Isn't he the boy you played tennis with a couple of weeks ago?"

"Well, yes. But I don't want him coming over *here*." I threw down my back and kicked it into the corner.

"Why not? I'd like to meet him. Isn't his brother seeing your friend Natasha?"

"Yeah, well ..." I let the sentence hang. I looked around at our bulging house with its clutter of books and piles of newspapers and K-mart catalogues; the dog leads dangling from a hook in the hall; the breakfast things still on the kitchen counter. I sniffed the air – over the top of Eau de Dog, hung a whiff of last night's lamb roast. "Why's he coming over here? I thought we were going to practise at school."

"Ms Carlton said that both the library and auditorium had been double-booked and that she was sorry. But she said that it was good practice for you. Here's his number. She wants you to call him and confirm arrangements."

I had to call him?

"He won't bite." Mum laughed and went back to the kitchen.

I mooched to my bedroom and when I'd run out of things to do, I sent him a text.

Hi Sam. Apparently, you're coming over to my place tomorrow.

Hi Lucy. Apparently so.

That was all he said? I stared at the screen and thought for a minute. I typed back,

Do you know where I live?

No.

I'll meet you at the station straight after school.

K

I threw the phone onto my bed and spied, underneath, a pair of leggings poking out. I knelt down to pull them out and discovered some old grape stems, a stripy sock, a Crunchie wrapper, a textbook from last year and my collection of rocks. I clambered up and dusted off my knees.

I am messy. Well, so what? Sam Curtis would have to have to take me as I was. I went back out to the kitchen.

"What do you want me to bake for afternoon tea tomorrow?" asked Mum.

"Why do you have to bake anything?"

"Well, Sam's coming over."

"So?"

"It's polite to offer guests food and drink," Mum said.

"Sam's not a guest."

"Yes, he is and boys are always hungry."

That was true. I had witnessed how my four male cousins behaved at the dinner table. It wasn't unheard of for the youngest to lick his hand and rub it all over the dish of baked potatoes so that his older brothers wouldn't get to them first. It was disgusting.

"Okay," I said, grudgingly. "You can bake something. Maybe your caramel slice. Sam likes chocolate."

I walked along the platform the following afternoon, looking for Sam. When I found him, he was yammering to a few mates with his hands deep in his pockets. His tie was loose and he'd rolled his sleeves to the elbows. From a distance, he looked more like Hugh than I'd ever noticed before. Sam spotted me and came over.

"Hey."

"Hi."

I know. Witty repartee.

"Guy I was just talking to reckons he's friends with a friend of yours. Brigitte."

"Really?" I didn't know Brigitte knew any boys apart from Scott Morgan, who didn't count, and I looked with interest at the guy. He had broad shoulders and was pretty fit looking. Nice. I didn't recognise him.

"Where's the charming Natasha? I thought you were glued at the hip."

"Um, she's somewhere round."

Sam grinned. "You haven't told her, have you?"

"Sure I have." I tossed my hair back.

"No, you haven't."

"It's just that she has a thing about debating."

"And me."

"Not at all. She loves you. No, I don't mean it that way," backpedalling like crazy, "Not you. She loves your brother. No, wait. She thinks you're cute. Or rather we're cute together." Oh, god. Too late, I realised what I'd said. I could feel myself go bright red. I wanted the station to disappear me to Hogwarts. Sam just kept grinning. Thankfully the train arrived at the platform, preventing my motormouth making things even worse.

By the time we arrived at my station, I'd gotten myself together. It took about 15 minutes to walk home and for most of it I managed to keep our conversation restricted to the weather and when we'd exhausted that subject moved on to school. I found out Sam was a good storyteller.

"I've got this crazy German teacher, right? He's quite large. Always speaks German with a really heavy accent so we call him Schultzy. This guy in my class, Baz, couldn't get this verb right – he's always stuffing up; never does his homework, it drives Schultzy crazy, bonkers – and he kept saying it over and over again until Schultzy rapped him over his knuckles with a ruler. Baz has really quick reflexes, he's in the cricket team, and before Schultzy could do anything he grabbed the ruler and broke it in half. Schultzy then slammed his hand onto the desk, really, really hard, right, and shouted Baz's name so loud that Baz went over backwards on his chair. Schultzy, he's really big – did I tell you that? – he hauls Baz up by his arm and shakes him, right, really, really hard so that you could hear Baz's teeth rattling around in his head. You should have seen Schultzy's face: it was almost purple and all contorted with rage and he was sort of puffing. I thought he was going to hit Baz. Either that or have a heart attack. Someone said 'Sir' in a loud voice and that brought him to his senses. He dropped Baz's arms. Baz was shaking and this is a guy who once played a match with a dislocated shoulder. Luckily the bell went and we got him out of there quick smart."

"Nothing like that ever happens at my school." I sounded rueful. "Once we made our French teacher cry, but that wasn't anything. Ms King can cry just looking at a poster of the Eiffel Tower."

"Can't win them all," said Sam wisely.

Mum had laid out a plate of caramel slice and two cups of orange juice for our afternoon tea, but wasn't anywhere in sight which made me grateful.

"Beware, the hounds of hell," I said to Sam as Sid and Nancy threw themselves at his legs. He patted them. "Vicious, aren't you?" he said to them as they prepared to lick his hand to death. He straightened up. "I didn't know you were into punk? I'm impressed."

"Why do you think that?"

"You named your dogs after two punk rockers," said Sam, patiently.

"Oh, that. That was my dad. I'm more into regular music. What about you? Put your bag here," I said, "and come through."

He eyeballed the slice straightaway. "Yeah, I'm into punk. It's intense and way better than poetry or rap. Can I have some of that?"

I pushed the plate towards him,

He was onto his third piece when Mum, dishevelled and damp in her gardening slacks and shirt, banged through the wire backdoor. Her wide-brimmed hat became caught in the door, pulling her up short. In the end she ducked and ignored the dangling hat.

"You must be Sam," she said, with as much dignity as she could muster.

"Pleased to meet you, Mrs Johnson," said Sam. "Did you make this slice? It's awesome."

Mum set down the secateurs and removed her gardening gloves. "I was under Lucy's instructions, dear. She said that you particularly liked chocolate."

Sam nodded, his mouth full of slice.

"Would you pour me a glass of water, Lucy? I'm too dirty as I am."

Mum drank two glasses quickly, put the empty glass in the sink, picked up her gloves and secateurs and opened the door, catching her hat as it fell. She jammed it on her head. "Righto, aphids wait for no man or woman." She disappeared the way she came, nearly tripping over the wriggling dogs at her feet.

"If your mum fights aphids the way she cooks, there'll be a massacre."

"Is that your fourth piece, Sam Curtis? I don't believe it."

I looked him up and down, taking in his lankiness. Where did it all go? He just grinned and when he was finished he leaned against the kitchen sink, his arms folded and waited.

"Will we work straightaway or do you want to hang out for a bit first?"

"Let's work first, play later."

So we set up books and our laptops on the dining room table and went to work. The question was: Should you go Dutch on the first date? We were debating the affirmative even though Sam thought that guys should pay for the first date.

"Don't you think that's a bit sexist?" I screwed up my nose.

"Why are you complaining? You're getting a free movie or dinner," Sam said.

"What if the girl then expects you to always pay?"

"I'd have to get a second job."

"I didn't know you had a first job."

"I clean the cages at the vet one afternoon a week."

"Is that okay?"

"Sure. The vet assistants are hilarious. They're always pranking the vet."

"Like how?" I pushed the laptop away from me and turned to face him.

"One time, they pretended that he'd just euthanised the wrong cat. They came running into theatre screaming, 'You've got the wrong cat. That one is in for worms.' He just about dropped the syringe."

"That's awful," I said.

"It is, isn't it?" Sam said, grinning. "Another time they sewed up the pockets on his coat."

"Do you want to be a vet?"

"Dunno. Maybe. My parents want Hugh and me to follow in their footsteps and be doctors."

"Your mum's a doctor, too?"

Sam nodded.

"Hmm," I said, "definitely a feminist. I bet she'd expect to go Dutch on a first date."

"Dunno, never asked her."

I pulled the computer closer and began to type, 'I think that girls shouldn't expect the guy to always pay for stuff. I think it sets up bad habits. I think girls should be economically independent right from the start. Otherwise, they'll never learn.'

Sam, looking at the screen over my shoulder, said, "I'll have to remember that on our first date."

"Dream on, Curtis."

After about an hour, he stretched. "Reckon we've done enough?"

"Do you have to go or do you want to hang around?"

"Nah, I'll stick around for a while," he said. He pushed himself back from the table.

"So, what now?"

"Want to watch something? Or we could play Totem tennis."

"Totem. I haven't played that game for ages."

Milly's Totem tennis set was already set up on a scorched patch of buffalo near the clothesline. All we had to do was find some yellow bats.

"I gotta warn you, I'm an ace player," said Sam, lining up his first shot. It caught me in the eye. He dropped his bat and hurried over.

"God. Sorry, Lucy. Are you hurt?"

I gingerly removed my palm from my eye socket. "Is my eyeball still there?" I asked him. He crouched to peer into my face. "Two brown eyeballs. Check." His breath was warm with chocolate and his eyes were green as the wings of the lorikeets above.

"You'll have to do better than that if you want to win." Sam laughed and stepped away.

Later, we lay side by side on the grass, puffing and inhaling pittosporum spores. I had that faraway feeling you get when everything but you is oversized. The gum trees loomed over our heads and the clouds that scuttled past were enormous rabbits and ships. I heard the clip of a mynah's wings as it patrolled the airspace above our heads. Sam's left arm was close to mine and I could see his chest rise and fall from the corner of one eye. His other arm was resting under his head. I put a hank of hair to my mouth and spoke through it. "Have you ever wondered what's out there? In space."

"What? Like little green men?" Sam squinted at the sky.

"No, I mean, well, sort of. Sometimes at night, looking at the stars, I feel very small and I wonder if there's a parallel universe out there somewhere."

"There has to be. We can't be the only planet with life on it. Do you know we're basically made up of stardust? When the big bang happened the universe broke up into tiny pieces of matter that eventually became us."

"I like the idea of a star being part of us," I said. "There's definitely gotta be something else out there. There can't just be us." I turned my head to look at his profile. His fringe had fallen from his face and it made him look younger, more vulnerable. "Don't you wonder that sometimes?"

Sam shifted a bit and our arms brushed. "What if there's nothing out there at all. Just a big old black hole of nothing, lying in wait just beyond our solar system."

"You're a nihilistic punk lover. Basically, you're saying we're doomed," I said gloomily. "That's a cheerful thought."

"It is, isn't it." Sam plucked a blade of grass and chewed on it. "It means we'd better live life to the full while we can. YOLO."

"Isn't that just an excuse to do whatever you want? Like eat a whole packet of Tim Tams?"

"If the end of the world is coming, I'd want to do something a bit more meaningful than stuffing myself full of biscuits. What about a soundtrack to go with this apocalypse? *London's Burning?*"

"We're in Sydney," I said.

"*Doomsday Clock* by the Smashing Pumpkins?"

"Nice. Or what about *The Ride of the Valkyries?*"

"I think Coppola took that one already."

"Right. What about *The Earth Died Screaming?*"

"Tom Waits?" Sam said, nodding. "A classic. I like it. I didn't expect you to know that one."

"My dad," I explained. "He has eclectic taste in music."

"That's right. He loves punk. What a dude. I'm impressed." He really was.

"Wait," I said with my finger up. "I've thought of the best one: Robbie Williams' *Millennium.*"

He caught on quickly and laughed. "I forgot about him. I was about to suggest something by Busta Rhymes or Nine Inch Nails, but, no, you're right. Robbie Williams is the perfect choice for a modern day apocalypse. He's symbolic of everything that's wrong with Western civilisation."

"He's not the only one. I heard that oil tankers play Britney Spears on loud speakers so that Somalian pirates can't board. The pirates see her as an example of depraved western culture and won't step on a Britney-loving ship."

"I wouldn't board a ship playing Britney Spears, either."

"Want to play some music in my room?" I said. "I promise not to play anything as depraved as Britney."

"Well, all right, then," Sam said, and he stood and, in a gentlemanly gesture at odds with his loose tie and scruffy hair, held out his hand to me. And, you know what, it didn't feel hokey or stupid or an anti-feminist gesture.

"Thanks." I took his hand and he hauled me up. I thought for a second that he was going to groan like he was doing some seriously heavy lifting, but he didn't and I was weirdly pleased that he didn't make that a big joke, too.

"I'm going to treat you to both kinds of music: country and western." I plugged my laptop into a set of speakers that were see-through and filled with a light show that exploded in time to the music, one of my most treasured possessions.

"Cool speakers," said Sam. "What else have you got?" He wandered around my messy room peering at my stuff: the beads slung across the edge of the mirror, the silver dog, the cactus plant on my dresser and the positive affirmations stuck on the wall. He laughed at a cartoon I'd put up of a fairy-tale princess climbing out of a tower by using a ladder labelled 'corporate'. He also looked at the photos. The picture of Sid and Nancy as puppies sitting inside Dad's old sneakers, a family photo snapped in front of the Big Pineapple, and a picture I'd printed out of Natasha and me in which our skin is as bleached as our teeth. Not the most flattering so I was a bit put out that he looked at that picture the longest. At least he didn't comment on how messy my room was.

"We're going to start with Maclamore," I announced loudly.

"Mmmm," murmured Sam. He'd moved on to the bookshelf. You could tell a lot about a person by the books they read. I hoped that my Lemony Snicket collection would stand up to scrutiny.

"You've got this," he said, pulling out *The Hitchhiker's Guide to the Galaxy.*

"You don't have to sound so surprised. Girls read science fiction, too, you know. Just for your information, *Doctor Who* is one of my favourite shows on television."

"Mine, too. What's your favourite episode?"

"The angels with teeth. Definitely."

"Wow. Mine, too."

"Who's your favourite Doctor?"

"Not the latest, that's for sure."

"Me, too."

We high-fived on the down-low.

We'd been sitting on the floor of my bedroom, our backs against my bed for about half an hour listening to Dolly Parton and talking about our favourite books when Sam stirred. "Suppose I'd better go. Still got that German homework to do."

I flicked off Spotify and nodded. "Thanks for coming over."

"Thanks for asking me," said Sam.

"You're welcome."

We smiled at one another.

"Okay, then," Sam picked up his bag on his way out.

"Say bye to your mum for me," he said.

"Are you going, Sam?" The voice came from behind one of the rose bushes on either side of the front door.

Sam took a step back. "Whoa. Is that you, Mrs Johnson? Thanks for the slice."

"You're welcome. We'll see you at the debate."

"Yep," he said.

We stood at the letterbox while Sam scuffed his shoes on the stone path. He seemed reluctant to go.

"Goodbye then." He finally started off up the street.

"Wait," I called out. He turned.

"Thanks for doing all this," I said.

"Same to you. We're a great team."

Then he said, "Watch out for Nick at the dinner dance."

"How did you know about that?" I said.

"How do you think? Guys talk, too, you know."

Suddenly I wasn't smiling anymore and neither was he.

Chapter 22

"Sam seems nice," said Mum the following night at dinner. "But ... have I got this straight? You're going to a dinner dance with someone else?"

I kept my head down over my bowl. It was Friday, Aunt Gert was over, and she was all ears.

"About the dinner dance: Mum, it might be better if Nick picks me up from Natasha's house."

"I see," said Mum, but she patted her hair like she didn't, so I hurried on. "Hugh lives next door and we're sort of all going together. Natasha said I could stay the night, too. So, you won't have to stay up to collect me or anything."

"I suppose that makes sense," Mum said slowly. "What do you think, Doug?"

Dad pushed at his glasses. "That means we won't see her before her first dinner dance."

Mum sniffed. "Our little girl is growing up."

"Hooey," said Aunt Gert. "That little girl of yours has been a woman for some time, Maureen. You've just never noticed it. Tell me, Lucy. Are you planning to French kiss your young man at the dance?"

"Good grief," said Dad, taking another gulp of his drink.

"Aunt Gert!" said everyone else in the room. Except Milly, who asked in an interested voice, "What's a French kiss?"

"Don't you dare," said Dad in a steely tone to Aunt Gert.

"What? Don't look at me like that, Doug. Modern girls these days know all sorts of tricks. And if Lucy doesn't, then she'd better learn."

"Good Lord," said Mum, reaching for her glass of chardonnay.

"I barely even know the guy," I spluttered. Geez Louise. How did my love life end up being discussed this loudly at the table?

"So, it's a blind date," said Aunt Gert with interest. "That's the only dating I do now. Two blind people going on a date." Aunt Gert sighed. "My dates don't last long, either. Mr Salvio nods off as soon as the dinner plates are cleared."

"Isn't it about time to take Aunt Gert home?" I stared meaningfully at Dad.

"Is it? But I haven't finished my soup." said Aunt Gert and, thankfully, returned to it.

Later, I helped Gert out to the car by carrying her giant carpet bag.

"What have you got in there? A corpse?"

She sniggered as she tottered towards the car. At the door, she paused.

"Here, take this," she said, and palmed me a $20. "Buy yourself something nice to wear."

What century did she think this was? For $20 I'd only be able to buy the mascara. Still, it was very thoughtful of her and I squeezed her gratefully.

"Hey, watch you don't knock me down," said Aunt Gert. "I'm not too steady on my pins these days."

She winked at me as Dad lowered her into the car. "We sirens have to stick together."

"Don't we just." I could still hear her titter as I shut the car door, leaving her hem poking through.

Mum put her arm around me as we walked back inside.

"I'll do the washing up," she said. "You go finish your homework."

Before I could make a start, my phone went off. It was Natasha.

Want 2 no wat I am wearing 2 dinner dance?

For the next ten minutes there was a flurry of texts about the pros and cons of silver highlights against her blonde hair and whether she should put it up.

Then my dad came into the room to take my phone and put it on the charger for the night. It was a family rule. No electronic gadgets in our rooms after 8pm.

After I'd done that I realised we'd spent so long on her outfit, we hadn't figured out what I'd wear.

I went to find Mum, who instantly recognised a crisis when she saw one, springing into action with the resourcefulness of the country girl she once was. She found an old pink satin T-shirt that she'd saved from my throw-out pile last year and a pile of fluffy soft netting that she had been meaning to turn into a mosquito net for Milly's bed. She gathered it up, instead, into layered clouds of delicate colour and fastened it to a silky waistband in a pink as rich as the T-shirt. Not quite full length, it grazed my ankles and spilled out beneath the tight T-shirt. It was subtle, whimsical and exquisite.

I'm thinking about ballet flats. Thoughts?

It was Saturday morning and I texted Natasha. I'd already decided to wear ballet flats not high heels but I wanted her approval. It was either ballet flats or combat boots – an ironic gesture that I knew Sam would get. Except that I wasn't going with Sam. I was going with another guy – the perfect guy. No way I could concentrate on homework I hadn't yet touched or next week's exams that I hadn't prepared for. No, right now it was far more important to get the outfit right for the perfect date with the perfect guy. Natasha's answer when it came through was scathing.

What are you? The sugar plum fairy? Got 2 wear heels. The bigger the better.

But a contrariness had taken hold of me. I borrowed a pair of ballet slippers that were being saved for Milly when she grew. They were in a delicate pale pink and all I had to do was paint them silver. I used Gert's money to buy the fabric paint.

By Saturday afternoon, my outfit was hanging on one of mum's padded coathangers. The silver slippers lay side by side underneath, so pretty Hans Christian Andersen would have approved. But what about Nick Hall? What if he'd prefer a more sophisticated, glamorous date – a model, say, like his ex? Or someone who looked like she might 'put out' at the end of the night: someone more like Amanda or Lindsay.

I'd heard Amanda describe what she was wearing to the dinner dance and she sure wasn't aiming for 'pretty'. Stretchy, revealing and tight were adjectives she used and perfect for a limousine tryst. She wasn't a virgin, either, or so she liked to brag in the change room before gym, discussing it like she was talking about opening a packet of Smith's chips.

This was all I could focus on in the car on the way over to Natasha's that afternoon, my knees pressed firmly together, my ballet flats in my bag along with my T-shirt and pyjamas. And all the while Mum, in typical fashion, was droning on about the mundane, the practical. 'Have you got your phone? Keep any flowers so that I can press them later. And don't forget to thank Mr Fielding for taking you', until I wanted to leap off a bridge.

You'd think that mothers would get tired of saying all that crap, I thought as I jumped out, pulling out my overnight bag, and shutting the car door firmly which cut off a sentence that began with "Take lots of photos. I want …"

"Bye, Mum," I mouthed. "Thanks for the lift."

What there wouldn't be would be photographs. Then Lindsay would realise that two of her best friends were really traitors of the worst kind.

How we'd managed to keep Lindsay in the dark for six whole days, I would never know. There were a couple of very close calls. One time, Lindsay came up when Natasha was describing her dress to me. Another time, Lindsay began to grill Natasha on why Nick had changed his mind and who was he taking, anyway? Amazingly, Natasha still didn't cave.

Me? I would have broken down then and there and confessed to everything and more. Not Natasha. That girl had nerves of steel. She just shrugged and said, "Hugh's begged Nick to change his mind, but apparently, his father is making him take his cousin. I feel *sorry* for Nick." Lindsay didn't say any more, but more than once I caught her looking at Natasha and me with a frown like she wasn't really buying it.

Well, I wouldn't think about that. Focus on the positive. That was the key. There I was, Lucy Johnson, going to a dinner dance with an older guy, and not just any older guy, but one of the hottest boys at Northcote Grammar. It was social nirvana. What's more, I was double-dating with the most popular girl at my school, and we were getting ready *together*.

Natasha, when she'd emerged from the bathroom just before five o'clock, where she'd been for the past hour, certainly was focusing on the positive in a white sheath dress.

"You look a-maz-ing. Hugh is going to literally *die* when he sees you."

She smiled gracefully, then wrinkled her brow. "Are you sure I don't look too fat in this?"

"No way. Nuh uh. A pretzel." Beside her I felt like an oversized fairy. Natasha blotted her lipstick for the second time and tipped her head upside down to shake her golden tresses out so that they fell about her shoulders – lightly tanned by Ella Baché – in a glossy curtain down her back.

I had also kept my hair out, but I had fastened pieces from the side in tiny clips that I had borrowed from Milly. In my house in front of my adoring sister I blossomed and sparkled. Next to the drop-dead gorgeousness of Natasha, I wilted. When he sees me,

Nick is going to wish that he had taken Lindsay, after all.

The doorbell rang at five sharp.

"Daaad. Can you get that? It'll be Nick and Hugh. Tell them we aren't nearly ready." Natasha was re-doing her barely there eye make-up.

I heard Mr Fielding answer the door. He walked past the bathroom a little while later.

"Did you tell them, Dad? Where are they? Did you put them in the lounge room? Offer them a drink?" Natasha squealed when he told her he'd left them at the front door – "Daad, you're hopeless," – and ran down the hall, flinging open the front door. I moved in behind her. I could hear Mr Fielding in the background.

"Gotta keep the young bulls on their toes."

Nick and Hugh stood together on the driveway, sweating in the late afternoon sun in suits hired for $200 a night. Hugh's eyes darkened as soon as he saw Natasha standing in the doorway. He made a throaty sound. "Get over here," he said and he pulled her to him. Nick lifted an eyebrow at me. My stomach was full of blowflies, my mouth dry as cotton.

"You look like the good witch of the south. What's her name?"

"Glinda."

"Yeah, Glinda."

At least I didn't look like Angelina Ballerina.

With cool irony he handed me an orchid cuff and brushed my cheek with a kiss like fairy floss. When he stepped back I saw that he was wearing not suit trousers but black jeans and sneakers. His tie was unravelled, his hair messy like he'd just run his fingers through it.

"Hey. Like your deconstruction of the suit – very retro," I said. His lips went up at the edges, but not quite enough to be a smile and I began to feel a bit shaky and unsure.

Natasha and Hugh pulled apart and Hugh opened the box he held for Natasha. I watched him slowly push it onto her wrist.

"Daad, we're ready to go," called out Natasha.

"It's really nice of you to drive us," said Hugh, politely as Mr Fielding reappeared, jiggling the car keys in his pocket. "Dad was going to but he had to go away to a conference at the last minute."

"Just make sure you bring home my daughter in one piece," said Mr Fielding, eyeballing him.

"You bet, sir. We'll get an Uber," said Hugh.

Just then Sam came home, strolling down his driveway with a sports bag in his hand. He ceased whistling, halted and saluted his brother and Nick. "Hey."

Hugh nodded to him. Nick said, "Yeah. S'up?"

Sam's glance took in Natasha and me. He pursed his lips in a silent whistle and said, "Wow." Our eyes locked. I looked away first. I wished that he hadn't seen us. He nodded to Nick. "Have a good one."

Nick gave him a look that said he sure would. Sam stiffened and walked inside.

Chapter 23

Northcote Boys Grammar had taken over the main function room of the golf club. There were 20 round tables, each set for 10 and arranged around a wooden stage and floating wooden floor. A bunch of black and white helium balloons were anchored to tiny sandbags in the centre of each table, along with jugs of orange juice and chilled water that were already lukewarm.

A new waiter – thank god Scott Morgan had gone – stood in the doorway holding out a tray of soft drinks. We took one and made our way out to the terrace. The long shadows of the trees edged their way along the fairway of the first tee, stretching all the way to the bunker.

A sheet with the names of each table was set up on a stand and Natasha, holding her hair back from her neck, ran her finger down the list looking for ours. There we were: Hugh Curtis and Natasha Fielding. Nick Hall and Lucy Johnson.

"I've heard his ex-girlfriend is going to be here," said Natasha, leaning in so that we couldn't be heard.

"Really?" I looked around.

"Yeah, Racquel Richards. She's a year ahead of us at school. Have you seen the latest Pavement ad? She's in that. She was discovered at Hornsby shopping centre last year by a talent scout. I've heard she's going to be in the next Bonds catalogue. Look – she's sitting at our table." She tapped her finger against the page, "I wonder who she's here with?"

I didn't catch sight of Racquel until we were being seated for dinner and Deborah was serving the tables baskets of bread rolls.

"Hi, Lucy," she said. "Not working tonight?"

"Ah, no, not tonight Deborah." I ducked my head, glad that Nick had jumped up to say hi to some guys out on the terrace and hadn't overheard. I looked around for Natasha and Hugh, both of whom had disappeared in the vicinity of the locker rooms.

"Hi, I'm Toby Tulloch." A tall boy with a broad forehead and a big Adam's apple collapsed into the chair next to mine.

"Hi, Lucy Johnson."

"All alone?"

I blinked up at him. "Aren't we all?"

"That's a bit heavy for a party," he said. He poured water into his glass and mine and leaned for the bread basket. "Do you want yours?" and taking two before I had a chance to say 'No.'

"Right," he slapped his hands jovially on his thighs. He stretched to read the name place of my date. "Who are you here with?" He made a low whistling sound when he read the name tag, and checked me out more thoroughly. "You don't look his type. No offence."

"None taken," I said, dryly.

"I meant that you look too normal for him." He looked around. "So, where is the old Nickstar?"

"No idea." I took a sip of water. "Who are you here with?"

"Racquel Richards."

Ahh. That was why Toby was so worried about where Nick was. I scanned the room, looking for her. Toby saw.

"She's in the bathroom. As always."

I nodded. If I was a model like her, I'd spend a lot of time in front of a mirror, too. Nick dropped into the chair beside me. "There you are." As if I had been the one to go missing.

"You and Tobes have met," he said, banging Toby on the shoulder. "Mate, look after her, would you."

I thought at first he was talking about me. Then I saw a thin, pale, pretty girl in a little black dress staggering towards our table and I knew he meant her: Racquel Richards, the model and his ex-girlfriend.

"Hi, Nick," she said. She ignored Toby and me, and sat down close to Nick.

"Racquel," Toby said. "Have you met Lucy? She's Nick's date."

She looked at me as if I was a bug on her shoe.

Later, after the plates had been cleared, Natasha reached across Hugh's chest to draw his phone from his inside pocket. "Coming?" she said to me. We went outside to the terrace and in the soft evening struck provocative poses while she took selfies, as, she said, "a little surprise" for Hugh later.

"Aren't you scared Hugh's parents might see them?"

"No." She rested one slender arm, the one with the phone, on my shoulder and took sexy shot after sexy shot. Or, rather, she was sexy. I stood there looking like a drip.

"Are we ready to go back in?"

Natasha shook out her hair and straightened her dress. "Nearly."

As we headed inside to join the dancing, Natasha paused. "Did you know Racquel tried to get back with Nick tonight?"

"What did he say?"

Natasha shrugged. "Who cares? Let's dance."

Later, I pushed my way out of the double doors at the foyer of the golf club and into the car park. I was hot and wanted to cool off. I held my arms above my head. I could hear the thud, thud of the bass inside the partly open doors and waved my upstretched arms in time to it.

"Hey, Lucy."

I dropped my arms and turned to see Nick watching me.

"What are you doing with your arms?"

"Nothing." I couldn't possibly tell him I was dancing by myself like a loser. "Anyway, let's go back inside." I gave a little enthusiastic shimmy. "I love this song."

He laughed and a second later I knew why. The song that had just started up – Shania Twain's *Man! I Feel Like a Woman* – was probably the worst song ever. I felt my cheeks burn.

"You're adorable." He stepped into me and leaned down to put his mouth on mine. The kiss went on long enough for me to think, 'Wow, I'm kissing Nick Hall.'

"What's going on?"

At the sound of Natasha's voice, I felt him pull away. And there she was wedged under Hugh's arm with his jacket over her shoulders. Her mouth was curled up in a derisive smile. I hadn't heard their footsteps on the gravel.

Nick straightened up and took a packet of cigarettes out of his pocket. He offered them up. Hugh shook his head. "In training," he said, but Natasha took one and held Nick's wrist steady with her hand as he lowered his head to light it for her. I didn't know she smoked.

"Thanks," she said, her glance skimming over him. She exhaled smoke, thoughtfully, with her head slightly tilted so that the spotlight under the cool eaves of the golf club captured the lovely planes of her face. Hugh, watching her, did so in a way that every girl longed for. I turned away and watched Nick strew little stones with a casual foot, and they rattled away. It was hard to imagine that just a few moments before Nick Hall had his lips on mine.

We stood there, the four of us, under a blanket of blinking stars, the freshly mown lawns around us disappearing into a velvety, balmy darkness. I was cold, but tried not to show it by holding myself stiffly. Beneath the acrid smell of smoke, I could almost taste the bubble-gum fragrance that drifted from the flowering hedges. Hugh and Natasha, still with his dinner jacket about her shoulders, were standing so close that a blonde strand of her hair became caught in one of his cufflinks. Nick and I were also side by side, not so close, but I was very aware of him, his restlessness. Would he kiss me again?

Eventually, Natasha ground out her butt with the sole of a stiletto.

"Let's go back in."

When Hugh opened the double doors, the music escaped like an exploding firecracker. He pushed into the room with Natasha holding fast to his hand, his jacket slipping off her shoulder to reveal a white strap. As I went to follow, Nick stopped me. His hand slipped around the back of my neck and he lowered his mouth to mine in an almost kiss. "I'll call you" and he was gone. Alone, I stepped back into the hall.

"Where have you all been? You're missing all the action," Toby bounded up. "Is Racquel with you?"

Hugh shook his head. "No, man."

Toby looked past Hugh's shoulder. "What about Nick?"

"He was here a minute ago," said Hugh.

"It's going *off*, man." Toby punched the air. "Conga, conga."

Natasha said. "Let's get out of here before he makes us join in." She looked meaningfully at Hugh. "Somewhere else, somewhere quiet. What about the oval?"

"I'd better stay, make sure he gets home." Hugh nodded towards Toby. "I'll call you a cab."

Natasha's face tightened. "Don't bother. Coming, Lucy?"

I gave Hugh an apologetic smile, nodded and followed her out.

Natasha stomped up to the main road, hopping mad, with me trailing along behind. "He can't do this to me."

I was confused. What exactly had he done? I said: "Don't you think it would be better to call an Uber or, maybe, a cab from the golf club?" I was huffing to keep up.

"Just hurry up, would you," she fumed.

When we got to the main road, she simmered down, pulling Hugh's jacket closer around her. I wasn't wearing anything warm, and shivered, feeling sick with tiredness. I wished we'd stayed at the golf club, got a taxi, a lift, done anything except walk up to the main road where the few cars around sped past, a blaze of headlights and rushing air. I felt creeped out here on the highway.

"What's the story with you and Nick?" Natasha made it sound like I'd committed a crime. It was only a kiss. Or was it? Could Nick Hall really be interested in me? I didn't dare believe it. But I didn't want to have this conversation with Natasha, not when she was acting like this so I stayed silent.

"He's out of your league, Lucy. I'm only saying that so you don't get your hopes up. I don't want you to get hurt."

Natasha stumbled a bit on the road. I laid a hand on her arm in an attempt to steady her. She shook it off which made Hugh's jacket slip off. She hiked it back up with a grumble.

"What's wrong?" I said. "Is it Hugh? I thought you guys were getting on really well."

"I've just gotta get out of here." She stuck out her thumb. I slapped her hand down. "Are you crazy? What if we get picked up?"

"That's the idea," said Natasha and sort of laughed. The next thing, there was a screech, and a Jeep with a red P plate flapping around on the bumper, pulled up. The driver, a cute surfie with bleached blond hair, leaned across his buddy to wind down the window. "What are two girls like you doing on a road like this? Hop in."

The car engulfed us and took off as soon as we sat down, me awkwardly hitting my hip on the chrome door handle. "We shouldn't be doing this," I said. But my words became tangled in the wind and the blaring stereo and the sound of the brakes as we turned off, hard, towards the oval.

It all happened so fast. I wasn't scared, though. Even when we'd parked the Jeep in the empty car park and the driver and Natasha walked away, Natasha swaying in her white sheath, his arm hooked around her neck. I merely sat there, waiting for her to come back. It didn't occur to me to fetch her or even to be worried for her safety. They were just a couple of years older than us, still boys even though they were driving. I stared at the scruff of the neck in the front seat. The tips of his hair were yellow white. I wondered if he'd used peroxide. Eventually, he turned around and I saw that he was younger than his mate, probably only a year older than me.

"Want me to join you in the back," he said, but without much hope.

"No, thanks." I pressed my lips and my knees firmly together.

So, we sat there in the dark, him in the front and me in the back in my sugarplum fairy dress with Hugh's jacket across my lap, not speaking and waiting for the other two to reaappear from the toilet block with its lewd graffiti and discarded beer bottles.

So, this was the oval at night, I thought, taking in the glowing toilet block, the broken floodlights and sordid dark edges of the playing field. Somehow, it wasn't as glamorous and exciting as I thought it would be.

Natasha and the other guy finally returned. They dropped us at the end of Natasha's street and we took off our shoes to walk the rest of the way home. Streetlights made it possible to see even though it was late, probably close to two or three in the morning. I remembered, too late, that I'd left Hugh's $200-a-night jacket in the Jeep. It was only then that my heart started thumping at the thought of what might have happened. I squeezed my eyes shut and saw the headlines. The bodies of two schoolgirls have been found in scrub in the bush near the oval. Beautiful, had their whole lives ahead of them, best friends ...

All the lights were off at Natasha's house. Next door's lights were out, too. I wondered if Hugh had come home yet. Would he be mad about his jacket? I stubbed my toe on the wooden verandah.

"Shh. Don't wake Dad," said Natasha, fiddling with her key in the lock.

She didn't seem so mad now, but there was a funny tightness around her mouth as she got ready for bed, taking off her bra through the sleeve of her sleep T-shirt and brushing her teeth with rapid strokes.

"What's that on your neck?"

"What?" Natasha looked closer at it in the mirror. "Oh, that. A hicky."

I wanted to ask her what had happened in the toilet block with the blond driver, but didn't know how to bring it up. Finally, I said: "You were gone for ages. What were you doing?"

"Oh, grow up Lucy. What do you think?"

Chapter 24

Monday morning Lindsay followed us after class as we headed down the path to the canteen. Natasha made room for her, but kept walking. Lindsay yanked on Natasha's arm, hard, until we all came to a standstill. She wasn't going to be ignored. When she removed her hand, the imprint of three of her fingers and her thumb remained behind as forensic evidence of an insecure girl becoming unhinged. Natasha looked at her arm and then at Lindsay.

"What are you doing?"

"I saw that picture of you at the dinner dance." Lindsay's protruding eyes were moist with emotion. What picture? I looked from Natasha to Lindsay.

Then I remembered the shots we took with Hugh's phone on the terrace. I looked with alarm at Natasha, who gave an imperceptible shrug.

"So, what was Lucy doing there?"

"She was there with Nick." Natasha gave me up in the blink of an eye.

"So, not a cousin, then." She turned her back on me. "Did you have a good time?"

"So-so," said Natasha. Standing beside her, I could only gape. We joined the snaking line of shrieking girls waiting to be served.

Putting a finger in her ear, Natasha said, "I can't stand this. Get me something?"

"Sure," I said. She didn't do queues, I knew that.

I was left alone with Lindsay.

"Natasha is only using you." She said it with spite. "She needs to pass her exams. Her dad is going to pull her out if she doesn't."

It wasn't true. She's just jealous, I told myself. She wasn't Natasha's best friend anymore and it was driving her crazy. I shook my head.

"Believe what you want." Lindsay put her hands on her hips, "Let me ask you this: whose house am I staying at on Saturday night?" She gave me a sly smile and pushed her way to the front of the line, leaving me behind at the rear.

"I don't know why Nick took Lucy instead of me?" I heard her voice over the chatter around me.

"Who does she think she is. All I know is, she'd better watch out. I'm onto her."

Suddenly afraid, I hustled behind a girl with a thyroid problem and crooked pigtails. She deserved better. I knew that. Up the front, I heard a girl – Emma, I think – attempt to placate Lindsay.

"What do you want? I'll get it for you."

"I don't think I could eat a thing. Maybe, umm, just a Mars Bar and a packet of salt and vinegar chips and a choccy Oak."

Emma pocketed the change and handed the food to Lindsay – her consolation prize.

"Thanks, I owe you," said Lindsay. She wedged the drink in her armpit and tore open the packet of chips with her teeth. "All I want to know is why?" She offered the packet to Emma as they elbowed their way back through the line. "But I'll pay her back: you can trust me on that."

I cringed behind Thyroid Girl, hoping not to be seen by Lindsay and Emma as they walked away from the canteen.

"Can I help you, dearie?" said the florid-faced canteen lady. I needed to pull myself together. I took a steadying breath, "A bag of vegetables, an apple and one muffin, please," and handed over my emergency money – being threatened constituted an emergency. But the muffin made greasy marks on the brown paper and, suddenly, I wasn't hungry any more.

I threw it in the nearest bin where it dropped like a stone to the bottom. I needed to find Natasha before Lindsay and Emma got to her.

I found her sitting on one of the park benches behind the tennis courts, her long legs resting on the seat opposite, her eyes closed and her face tilted to the sun. She looked relaxed and in control.

I flopped down beside her. "So, listen. Lindsay is going to get back at me for this."

"What are you yelling for? Chill." Natasha hadn't opened her eyes.

"Sorry."

"What did you get me?" Her eyes stayed closed.

I pulled the bag of cut-up carrots and cucumber from my pocket and laid it in her lap.

"What are we going to do?" I asked.

"About what?"

"Lindsay, of course."

"She'll get over it." Natasha straightened up, eyes opened. She picked out a stick of celery and took a bite. "What have you done to your hair? It looks really good."

"Oh, thanks." I touched my hair.

"Have you done your English questions?"

"Yes. Why?"

"I haven't. I'd better go and do them. Will you save me a seat? I'll probably be late coz of that."

"Yep. What will she do to me?"

"Who?"

"Lindsay." I practically screamed it. I mean, who else? Natasha's lack of concern was making me feel slightly unhinged.

"I'm more worried about Carlton. She hates anyone being late. I wish I'd had time to do them last night. But Dad was freaking out about the messy house and I had to do all these extra maths sheets. He was acting like a real control freak."

"Hey, you could copy out mine."

"Really? You wouldn't mind? You're the best." Natasha smiled warmly at me. I began to feel calmer.

I tried to stretch out my legs, but they weren't quite long enough. "What are we going to do about Lindsay?"

"Nothing. Like I said, she'll get over it." She pushed back her hair and I saw that my dolphin pendant was twisted around her wrist. "Carlton is threatening me with detention if I don't give it to her by the end of lunch. My book's in my locker. I'll give you the key." She pushed her shell pink nails into her tunic pocket. I took the key but didn't move.

"Um, do you think you could do it for me now?"

I blinked. "Oh, sure."

"Just put the folder back into my locker before the bell. Meet me tomorrow in the waiting room on platform two. Hugh and some of the other guys will be there. You can give me back the key then."

Did 'other guys' include Nick Hall?

As I got ready for bed later that night, I wondered if he'd call. Monday night was probably too soon. Tuesday or Wednesday, then? I pulled on my patchwork shorts and T-shirt with caped sleeves and the word Vague written across the chest in a parody of the magazine *Vogue*. They didn't match. Matching pyjamas were for little girls, not women of the world like me. When I was married to Nick, I probably wouldn't wear pyjamas at all. I'd go to bed naked or perhaps in a silk slip with velvet ribbon threaded in and out through the V at the front.

Milly came in to the bathroom as I was brushing my teeth. "Hey, Lucy. Aren't you going to play whist?"

I shook my head. "Hooork. Ahhh ot hoork."

"I'll let you choose trumps first." Milly put her cheek lovingly against my arm.

I took the toothbrush out of my mouth and spat. "I can't Milly. I've got to do homework."

"Poo. You're always using that as an excuse," said Milly. She put her head back on my arm. "Go on, pleeeze."

I gave Milly a friendly push out the door. "You start. I'll be there later."

I padded back into my bedroom and shut the door. After a few minutes, Mum knocked. Here we go.

"Lucy, why don't you want to play? Your dad's put out popcorn."

"Muuum, how old do you think I am?"

"Who's ever heard of being too old for card games? Aunt Gert is 83 and she still plays bridge."

I gave her a look. "She plays bingo and badly after all the sherries she's had."

"My point is we haven't seen much of you lately," said Mum. She pointed to the bed. "May I sit down?"

"It's a free country."

Mum raised an eyebrow. I muttered an apology and sat down beside her. May as well get the hormone talk over with.

"How was the dinner dance? You haven't talked much about it."

"Fine."

"Do you like Nick?"

"Mmmm."

"What does that mean?"

"It means I don't want to talk about it."

"Well, does he like you?"

"No! Yes! Oh, I don't know."

"But, he's the guy you're sweet on? Not Sam."

"Stop it. No one says that anymore."

"Sorry. Got the hots for, then."

"Sounds even worse. Better stick to 'sweet'. Or stop talking altogether."

"Is there anything you'd like to discuss or know?" she said.

"Nope. I just want to be left in peace to do my homework. I thought you'd be happy about that."

"Lucy, don't be ridiculous. All I'm trying to do is talk to you about what's important in your life."

"Well, thanks, anyway." I picked up my hairbrush. "Is that it?"

Apparently, it wasn't. Damn.

"I just want you to know that you don't ever have to do anything you don't want to."

"Does that include homework?"

"I'm trying to have a serious conversation with you about sex."

"God, Mum. I'm not having sex. Not with Nick or Sam or anyone else."

"That's great, darling. I just want you to know that you don't have to rush it. At your age, you can have a good, close relationship with a boy without it."

I shook my head. How embarrassing to talk about sex with your mother. And she kept going.

"Is there anything else bothering you?"

"Nope."

"We were very proud of you when you won this scholarship. My only concern is that you are feeling too much pressure. Are you?"

I shook my head again.

"You mustn't. Honestly. Aunt Gert has always supported your education; she insists on it and will keep helping out once Milly has started."

"I don't feel pressured. Actually, sometimes I do, but it's okay, Mum, I can handle it."

Mum took my hand. "You worry too much. You've always been a worrier. I remember a conversation I had to have with you about superannuation when you were about 10, Milly's age. Remember?"

I did. We were sitting at the kitchen table and I had a piece of paper and a calculator and I was working out the compound interest on my pocket money which was about 50 cents a week.

"You didn't finish your dinner tonight. Why?" Mum's question was asked in that seemingly casual way that mothers use when the answers mattered a great deal.

I snatched my hand away. "No! I'm not on a diet or about to die of anorexia. I wasn't very hungry, that's all." I clamped my mouth shut after that. I had to be careful with what I said. Mum had a way of winkling out the truth from me. I wasn't ready to discuss Natasha or Lindsay or what we'd done to her. I couldn't talk to her about Sam and how confusing our friendship was. I certainly didn't want to talk about my fantasy of being Mrs Nick Hall. She'd never understand.

Mum sighed and stood up. She smoothed down her clothes. "After you've done your homework we'd like you to come out to play at least one game. It's a family tradition and we'll miss you if you are not there."

"Yep," I reached for my book and pretended to read it until Mum left the room. I then lay across my bed, trying to read *I Capture the Castle*. How had Ms Carlton described it? An honest account of a young girl on the verge of life and love? I snapped the book shut. It was much too close for comfort. I could hear laughter from the living room.

Actually, I wouldn't mind playing cards. It would take my mind off those other things. I was feeling rather peckish, too, after having left most of my dinner.

I stood up. It wouldn't kill me to hang out with the family … it might even be fun.

Chapter 25

It was 8 on Tuesday morning, and the platform crawled with schoolies and commuters. Natasha and I had arranged to meet at the station and I approached the waiting room, pausing at the door. I was nervous about seeing Nick. Would he be able to tell that I had daydreamed that we were married? There were murmurings and some laughter. Good, there was a crowd. Imagine if it was just Nick and me in the waiting room. I'd just die. I glanced sideways to check I wasn't being watched – girls from our school were barred from loitering – and entered.

Natasha sat on Hugh's lap, brown legs swinging, chatting to Toby who was listening with his head down, grinning, legs stretched out and reddish blond hair poking up a bit at the back like he'd gone straight from the shower to the waiting room without bothering to check himself in the mirror. Just then Toby looked up and saw me. He gave me a salute with his forefinger. I tried to wave back, unsuccessfully as I juggled my school hat and my bag. Toby was okay even if he did punch the air with his fist and make conga lines. His top button was undone and his tie was poking out of his blazer pocket.

"Hi."

I plopped down next to him.

"Hi."

I tried to match his enthusiasm. He laughed. I laughed. Hey, this was going well. I went for a question next.

"Um, did you have a good time the other night? Y'know, at the dinner dance?"

"Yep, I did. How 'bout you? Last time I saw, you had some serious moves on the dance floor."

"Once the DJ got all the crap out of the way, he started playing good stuff."

Toby nodded. "Yeah, Eminem rocks."

I laughed. "I didn't mean him. Isn't he just a white boy pretending to be black?"

"Lucy's into Shania Twain." Nick emerged from the hazy corner of the waiting room, giving me one of those intense looks of his.

"No way."

But he was teasing me. I knew that. The air around me began to hum. He leaned against the door jam, looking out. His sleeves were rolled up and his tie was loose at the neck. I remembered our kiss. Would he keep his promise? I had to be careful not to show how much I wanted him to.

"I like your deconstruction of a school uniform."

"Thanks for noticing. I got up pretty early to get it just right."

He looked like he'd stayed up all night. He smiled at me and it felt like we were about to have a moment …

Toby muscled in. He clapped a hand on Nick's shoulder.

"This man here," he said, "Saved my arse the other night." He shook Nick's hand. "Thanks, man."

Nick didn't say anything. I looked at Toby to explain.

"Racquel was really losing it later on and he calmed her right down. Thanks for taking her home, man. She was acting way too crazy. I don't know how you did it for all those months."

"That's how he likes them." It was the first time Hugh had spoken since I'd arrived. Natasha still sat on his lap. Nick just flicked his cigarette butt out onto the tracks.

"Don't let the guard catch you doing that. You'll get us all busted," Hugh said. Natasha slithered off his legs. "Leave him alone. Can I bum a cigarette?"

Nick lit one for her. She inhaled, looking at him out of her cool blue eyes.

"Why do girls always fall for bad guys?" grumbled Toby. "What about guys like me?"

"Stupid, like you, you mean." said Nick. He grinned.

"I mean simple and uncomplicated." Toby grinned back. "Anyway, you're the stupid one for getting back with Racquel."

"Are you two back together?" Natasha flicked ash unconcernedly from her cigarette.

She might not care, but I felt stung, betrayed. Nick Hall had gone back to his girlfriend straight after kissing me! I got up to go. Natasha put out her hand. "Wait." I stopped, expecting her to collect her things and come with me. Girl solidarity and all that.

"Can I have my locker key?" was all she said.

"Sure." I took it out of my pocket and gave it to her. "Did you like what I did for the questions?"

"Didn't look at them, to be honest," she said. "But I'm sure they were brilliant." She turned to the boys. Toby was saying to Hugh, "That drop-kick friend of your brother's stole my phone."

"Who are you talking about? Paul?" said Natasha. "I met him at the informal a few weeks ago. I think Lucy kinda went for him."

"Oh, okay, well I'd tell her to watch out for him," said Toby. "I reckon he stole my phone. When I got home from your place the other day, I couldn't find it in my bag. I thought I must have left it at school, in my locker, but it wasn't there. I thought back to where I'd been: I had it at cricket, I know, because I was listening to it when I was waiting to bat. We then got a lift back to your place, remember? Yeah, well, your brother Sam was there and he had that loser friend of his over and they were playing COD in the games room. I put my bag down there to go to the kitchen. Remember?"

"We made those killer toasted sandwiches with the lot. Course I remember: it was only last week."

"Yeah, yeah. Well, I didn't have it when I got home, did I?"

"Are you sure it was Paul?" said Hugh.

"Well, it wasn't me. I don't think it was Sam. I mean, your brother is sometimes a little crazy but he's an okay guy. I've never known him to steal. I mean, he'll jump off the highest diving board at the pool or streak through the school for a dare. One time, he shoved a whole lot of balloons in someone's locker. Actually, that was pretty funny. Remember that? He did it to Lachlan Renshaw. Renshaw nearly died, you shoulda seen his face when all those balloons leapt out at him when he opened his locker at recess."

"Nah, it wouldn't be Sam. No way he'd steal from one of my friends. He knows I'd kill him if he did," said Hugh.

"It was Paul, I tell you. He's a bit of a dickhead at school. Always getting into fights and pushing his weight around," said Toby.

"Your train's coming," said Natasha. She'd moved to the door and was looking out. A tiny silver square grew longer and longer in the middle distance. She rested her back against the door jamb. "Listen. Toby, you said you were going to have a party next Saturday night. Well, are you?"

"Yeah, reckon. My parents are going away. You're invited. You too, Lucy. It's going to be huge."

Hugh's arm snaked around Natasha's waist and his lips were on her ear. "See you, babe," he said. "Bye, Lucy."

Natasha adjusted the jumper around her waist and dragged our bags with jerky movements to the doorway.

At school, I drank at the bubbler in slow gulps. Nick Hall was back with his ex. He was never interested in me. I don't know why I thought he was. I felt tears well up behind my eyes and I just made it to the toilet block before they came.

"What's wrong?" said Emma. She had followed me in and stood looking curiously at my reflection. I couldn't answer.

"You look really pale. Do you want me to take you to sick bay?" I was grateful for her concern.

"I can't be late for geography. Ms Bevans yelling at me is not what I need right now." My voice was wobbly.

Emma said, "Tell you what. I'll take you to sick bay then I'll go to class and tell Ms Bevans."

"Would you?" I wasn't ready to face the classroom looking all blotchy and upset.

"That's what friends are for." She put her arm through mine, gave it a squeeze. As she led me to sick bay, she began to probe.

"So, what's happened? Tell me everything. I won't tell anybody."

On that hot steamy Tuesday, two weeks before the end of term, with not a cloud in the sky, I told her. When I got to the part about Natasha and me keeping the fact that I went to the dinner with Nick from Lindsay, she breathed in slowly. "Tell me that part again."

Emma gently handed me over to Mrs Whitfield at the office for an ice pack and a cup of milky sweet tea served to me in a plastic cup so thin I burnt my fingers.

"What are your symptoms?" Mrs Whitfield put a manicured hand on the phone – "I'll ring your mother to collect you" – already pressing buttons. I shook my head at her, "No, don't. I'll be all right."

Mrs Whitfield put down the phone willingly. She didn't want the hassle of parents in her office. "Run along, then."

Emma had saved me a place beside her. "You haven't missed much."

The usually excitable Ms Bevans handed me her book, pointing to the place we were at, barely looking at me before turning to the blackboard.

"Thanks," I said, smiling gratefully at Emma, who smiled back.

The lunch bell rang. Emma and I found Natasha at the usual spot.

"What's up with you?" said Natasha.

"Nothing," I said, taking a bite of my sandwich. I knew Natasha had very little sympathy for me over Nick. Hadn't she told me already I was out of my league? Neither did she understand how I felt about betraying Lindsay. It was all right for her. Lindsay was hardly likely to take it out on Natasha. No, it was me she had in her sights.

"Your eyes are puffy," said Natasha. "Not a good look, especially if there's nothing wrong."

"But there is," said Emma. She turned to Natasha. "She told me everything," and she went on to tell it everyone else sitting with us: Kate, Sophie, Amanda, Kim, everyone.

"Shut up, Emma," I said. "I told you all this in confidence."

"It doesn't matter now," she said. "Everyone knows."

"Well that's because you told them." I put down my sandwich. I'd lost my appetite.

"Don't be mad," said Emma. "We're on your side."

"Really? Because it doesn't feel like it," I said. "Where is Lindsay, anyway?"

Natasha rolled her eyes. "Off sulking somewhere, I bet. Don't worry, she'll get over it once she finds out Toby is having a party on Saturday night."

"For real?"

The group of girls let out a collective gasp and that was the end of discussion about my broken heart and betrayal. I didn't know whether to be pleased or disappointed that I was already old news. I squinted into the distance and let the talk about the party wash over me. Brigitte and some girls were hanging on the netball courts. For the first time in ages I wished I was with them.

Chapter 26

Term one exams began on the same day as the morning radio host announced the beginning of a late unseasonal heatwave. Climate Change again. I couldn't believe how little I cared about the environment or the exams. Pass or fail, it didn't seem to matter. None of it mattered.

That morning, Mum packed ice bricks in our lunch boxes that melted before we'd even left the house. The heat had torn the colour from Mum's violets and roses in the garden so that they resembled exposed film.

At school the gym hall had been laid out with rows of desks and chairs. I sweated over science and geography papers, forgetting all I'd ever learned.

Outside afterwards, I dodged around the buzzing girls and their questions – "How was it?" "What did you put for question five?" "Did you finish?" – and shoved my books into my locker. I knew I'd probably failed and just wanted to go home and get this day over with. I don't know what made me glance into the bin as I hurried past. But I did and what I saw caused me to falter. Caught up between a paper bag and a chip packet was my dolphin necklace, discarded like a piece of rubbish. I scooped it up, quickly, before anybody noticed, and held it in my hand.

All the way home, I asked myself, why had Natasha thrown my precious necklace away amongst the lunch wrappings? Was it carelessness or an accident? Or was it that she didn't want it anymore? No! I couldn't believe that she might have thrown it away deliberately. I couldn't swallow the afternoon tea at home. I couldn't concentrate on reading my notes for tomorrow's exam. I sat at my desk sweating and feeling nauseous. By 5, it was so hot I abandoned my pretence of study and went out into the family room where Mum had fired up Aunt Gert's old portable air conditioner. It used up enough juice to power a small town so Dad banned its use except for emergencies.

"I'd say, mister, that 40 degrees constitutes an emergency. Don't you?" said Mum to the room in general and flicked the switch. The air conditioner which was the size of a refrigerator, made a noise like a truck driving down a train track at top speed.

It wasn't very relaxing, but being cool took priority over being able to hear or to think.

Milly and Mum shelled peas for dinner and I tried to organise my notes. Milly kept popping the peas in her mouth instead of the bowl and Mum kept yelling at her to stop it.

"What's the big deal? I'm eating my greens now instead of later," shouted Milly over the roar of the ancient air conditioner.

Mum couldn't argue with that so she turned on the television to find out when the heatwave was going to break. Headlines appeared in a stream across the bottom of the screen, which was good because we couldn't hear a thing. It flashed the headlines in bold red type: Seven Adelaide seniors broiled alive. Heatwave into record fifth day. Milly kept shovelling in peas like emergency rationing was imminent. Mum flicked off the television and went to the window. She gasped.

"You should feel the heat coming off this glass," she said. That was it. We took to the sofa with damp flannels on our heads. I got up only when my phone pinged. It was Natasha.

Call me.

I left the room, shutting the door behind me, and called Natasha.

"Hi, you told me to call you. What's up?"

"Finally," she said. "It took you long enough." There was no "how are you?", no "Sorry that I dragged you into this mess with Lindsay, no "I think I've misplaced the silver pendant you gave me." Instead, she gave me the news that the party was cancelled. Toby's parents were not going away after all.

"And I'd already put it up on Facebook," she wailed.

"You shouldn't have done that." I said, shortly. "You know what happened to that girl's house. It was trashed and the police were called. A car was driven into the pool!"

"I know. Amazing. I wished I'd been there," said Natasha. "What are you doing now? Can you come over?"

"We're supposed to be studying. We're in the middle of exams. Or hadn't you noticed?"

"What's up with you?" said Natasha. "You sound shitty."

"Sorry," I heaved a sigh. "I just can't get worked up about a party right now."

"You'll thank me later," said Natasha, "when you've helped me organise the party of the decade. Who knows? You might even hook up with someone."

I didn't bother to answer. If I couldn't have Nick, I didn't want anybody. Natasha didn't notice. "What about your place?"

Have the party here?

"You've got to be crazy," I said. "For a start, we're renting."

"So it won't matter if it gets trashed."

"Find another venue. I'm not having the party here. My parents would kill me."

My phone went silent.

"Natasha? Are you there?"

Natasha had hung up.

Natasha's second call came in at 8.15, after dinner was over and I'd taken a cold bath with ice from the ice machine in our fridge. Five more texts came through in 10-minute intervals, each one more desperate than the one before. Natasha was having it at her place. No she wasn't: her dad wouldn't let her. It was at the oval. No. Was I sure I couldn't host it?

"You've got to be kidding," I muttered under my breath. I didn't want my parents, who were sweating away in their underwear – Dad's Y-fronts in particular were spectacular in their tatty greyness and loose elastic – in front of the air con vent, to hear. I didn't bother calling back. She left 27 messages.

I picked up her 28th call.

"Think, Lucy. There's got to be somewhere." Natasha's voice was urgent. I couldn't quite see why it had suddenly become my job to find a party venue. Why wasn't Toby getting involved? He was the one supposed to be having the fricking party.

"I'll think about it some more," I promised.

"I'll meet you in the waiting room in the morning." Natasha hung up.

Chapter 27

On Thursday, the temperature had dropped to 18. Bizarre. I froze in my summer tunic on the station waiting for Natasha and *not* waiting for Nick to show up. As soon as she arrived, Natasha went to work.

"Pretty please." She draped herself over Hugh.

"No way," he said. "You're cute but why would I want to have the party at my place?"

"Well, why wouldn't you? All that fun. Anyway, it's either there or the oval."

"The oval's no good, man," said Toby. He'd just arrived and I moved aside to let him through. He dropped his backpack. "The police have been patrolling it."

"C'mon, pretty pleeeeze," Natasha nuzzled Hugh's neck. "Your parents are going out, you said so yourself."

"I'll organise it and everything," said Toby. "I feel really bad about it not being at my place."

"We'll help, too, won't we, Lucy?" Natasha hung on tightly even when Hugh pretended to throw her off.

"Bloody hell. All right."

"You mean it? Yippeee." Natasha threw her legs in the air.

"What have you got written there?" said Hugh, touching her thigh.

"The formulas for the maths exam today." She twitched her uniform triumphantly back into place. "Who cares about maths? We're going to have a party." She turned to me. "This calls for a trip to Northcote Mall this afternoon. We get off early because of exams."

"I have to spend some extra time on an extension paper," I said. "Will you wait for me?"

"Sure," she said. "We'll have Fro Yo".

Once again, I felt myself being sucked into her orbit.

We found a table at the back of Lemon Tree café: Emma, Lindsay, Natasha and I – the gang. Lindsay had told Emma who'd told me she'd forgiven me for stealing her date to the dinner dance. It wasn't as if he wanted to take me, either. He was just killing time until he got his girlfriend back. She shifted, in a magnanimous gesture, a couple of empty cups and saucers to a tray on the floor and wiped the table with a paper napkin before we sat down.

A bunch of guys, men, really, in T-shirts with the sleeves cut out to expose their ink were sitting at the table next to ours. They scraped out their chairs and leaned back to give us the slow once-over, not bothering to hide their interest. "Gotta love jail bait," I heard one of them say to his mate. Natasha flashed them a smile and then deliberately crossed her legs.

"Lucy, can you get us a couple of coffees. And some raisin toast. I'll pay you later."

It was quite the soiree, I noticed, as I returned with a tray of food, including cappuccinos with extra chocolate powder. I'd had to use the last of my emergency money and hoped Mum wouldn't ask about it. I knew I wouldn't get paid back.

The guys at the next table had pushed their chairs closer and were laughing about something Natasha had said. I set a coffee in front of her, wishing she hadn't got their attention.

"Hey, I know you," said one of the guys. I focused on him, startled. "You're … ahh … Linda, right?"

It was Scott Morgan.

"It's Lucy, actually," I said. "But, yeah."

"Wait. You know each other?" Natasha looked from me to Scott. "We work – worked – together at Northcote Golf Club," I explained as much for Scott's benefit as Natasha's.

Right, right," said Scott as realisation dawned. "'Sup?"

"Not much," I said sitting down.

The guys made ready to leave.

Natasha leaned over, "Hey, Scott, we're having a party later. You can come."

He gave her an appreciative look. "Sure. Why not?"

"See you *later*, gorgeous," said the tall one with a finger cocked at Natasha, who waggled her fingers back.

"Why did you do that?" I said to her, watching them climb into a Falcon with P plates parked on the street.

"What? Invite some hot guys to a cool party?" Emma shook her head like I was crazy.

"But they're, like, 18," I said.

"So what? They're hot." Natasha blew on her froth. "This is going to be the best party ever."

Natasha made a list on her phone. It was the invitation list. I saw that her name was at the top. Of course. Then mine. She wrote a bunch more. Emma, Lindsay, Hugh, Nick, Sam, Paul and half a dozen other names, all boys.

"Someone should make a playlist. I wonder …" She set aside the list to take a little sip of her coffee. A waitress, in sensible shoes and purple tights with a run in the back, began to clear the table next to ours, the one where the boys had sat. She tutted at the spread of opened sugar sachets. Natasha ignored her. "Who wants to hook up?"

Emma and Lindsay both nodded. Natasha put down her coffee.

"Lucy, do you?"

"Shhh, she'll hear us," I jerked my head in the direction of the waitress.

"You're avoiding the question. Well, do you?"

Emma and Lindsay leaned forward.

"Why would I want to do that?"

"Umm, because it's a party," Natasha made it a no-brainer – "and to get back at Nick."

That caught me by surprise. "Why would I want to do that?"

If I thought about it, he hadn't really done anything to me except invite me to the dinner dance, and he hadn't really even done that. He wasn't my boyfriend. The only one daydreaming about that was me.

"Why not?" Natasha made it sound a reasonable goal.

"Nah. I'm good."

"What about Sam?" Natasha said.

"What about him?" I looked around at everyone watching me closely. "We're just friends."

"So you keep saying," said Natasha.

Lindsay gave me a pitying look. "Whatever."

Natasha shoved Lindsay in the arm. "Leave her alone. It's not a crime to be clueless." Lindsay rubbed her arm and scowled. Natasha smiled brightly at me.

"Lucy Johnson, this party is going to be the most important night of your life. Trust me."

And she wouldn't leave it alone. Not even the next day as we headed down to school from the station. She called it her "finding me a 'friend with benefits' project".

"If not Sam, then what about Toby?"

Ewww. This was all wrong. What was I doing entertaining even the possibility finding a 'friend with benefits'. Wasn't it, like, having a boyfriend? But when I asked Natasha, she just laughed.

"You're so adorable, Lucy."

Personally, I didn't think so but Natasha had already moved on to the next candidate. Paul.

"No way!" Just hearing his name gave me the chills.

"Not going there again?"

"I never went there in the first place," I muttered.

"Nick Hall then. I mean, he's totally gorgeous."

I looked, open-mouthed, at her. Was she joking?

"I thought this was all in aid of getting him jealous or paying him back or whatever," I said.

"That's when I thought you had more, er, experience."

"Anyway, isn't he back with Racquel?"

"So what? They'll probably have split again by Saturday night." She laughed again. Then stopped to think. Finally, she said, "If you don't go for him, then we're back to Sam. He's pretty cute. Not in the same league as Nick, but all right looking. He's also Hugh's brother, so that gives him some cred."

But I'd had enough. "Stop it. This is my love life you're talking about. I get to have a say, don't I? And I say, 'no way'."

We were at school by now and approaching the lockers. Natasha shrugged. "Who said anything about love?"

I took a breath. "Me."

She rolled her eyes. I grabbed her by the arm. "Listen. You can't tell Sam about it. About this list. About me. Never."

"All right," Natasha pulled free. "Keep your panties on. God."

I didn't care what Natasha had in mind. I wasn't going to have sex for the first time at a party. I wanted it to be romantic and beautiful and with someone I loved. Not behind some stained couch with a billion people in the room, dancing around like they were at a fertility festival. Natasha loaded up her locker with books and checked her make-up in the little mirror that hung on the locker door.

"Sam and I are just *friends,*" I repeated.

"Get real," said Natasha, slamming her locker door shut. "Guys don't have girls for friends. They're only ever after one thing."

It wasn't until much later that I realised that Natasha hadn't asked me to stay over after the party. Perhaps Lindsay was right after all. Maybe Natasha had been using me all along to pass her exams and now that they were over she had no need for me.

I realised something else. I didn't care.

Chapter 28

Beep beep beep. It was 7am. Tomorrow had arrived. My hand shot out and slammed down on the clock's alarm button. I put on a pair of shorts and an old T-shirt that said *Byte Me*. I ate two Weet-Bix biscuits with skim milk. Sid and Nancy did their usual job of hoovering up the crumbs at Milly's feet. Mum pushed them away with her toe and as she stacked the dishwasher and asked the type of questions every parent always asked: What time will it finish? Who's going? Will there be adult supervision? Will alcohol be served?

I answered them flatly but honestly.

"I must say, you don't seem very excited about this party now that it's actually here."

"I think party's the wrong word. It's more of a gathering, really," I said. If my parents got wind of the fact that Natasha had put it up on Facebook, they'd never let me go.

"What are we talking about?" said Dad, strolling through the kitchen in his underpants and singlet.

"This 'gathering' that Lucy has been on the phone about for days organising," Mum said. "Am I right in thinking it's to celebrate the end of exams?"

"Sort of. Nice look, Dad," I said to change the subject.

"What can I say? Your old man has flair." He poured himself a glass of orange juice and then drank the rest straight from the container.

"Don't do that." Mum flicked him with a tea towel. "How old are you? Ten?"

Dad rubbed his thinning hair with one hand and dumped the container in the recycling bin with the other. "I look that young and incredible?"

Milly giggled. "That would make me, um, not even alive."

He grabbed her and began to tickle her. "I stay looking this young and fantastic by feeding on the flesh of little girls."

"Dad," Milly gasped, "Stop it." He let her go and turned his attention to me.

"What's a gathering? And explain to me how it differs from a party." He scratched his belly. "Because the way you've been glued to your phone makes it a party in my books."

I opened my mouth to explain the differences and promptly closed it. I'd only end up in hot water. Would they settle for "You wouldn't understand"? Probably not: these were my parents, after all; they called family meetings to discuss switching to low fat yoghurt.

But, really, what else could I say? I couldn't possibly tell them there'd be absolutely no adult supervision and that it had appeared on Facebook. They'd freak.

Even Year 12 students were planning to gatecrash it; Natasha, Lindsay and Emma had been planning their outfits for ages. They intended to be the hottest girls there. I had been part of the organising committee but I hadn't been invited to get ready beforehand or stay overnight next door. To be honest, I wasn't even sure I was still invited. I hadn't spoken to Sam in ages. Maybe it was for the best, since Natasha's insistence that he should be my 'friend with benefits' would probably only make me act weirdly around him.

"Is it going to rock?" Dad wasn't giving up.

I threw him a withering look. "You know your lingo is all wrong. Millennials never say that."

"Sorry, but I am a geologist."

"Daad. Sooo lame." I rolled my eyes.

"I'm also interested in what is going on in my daughter's life and trying to make a connection."

"I'm not sure I'm even going."

"But you've worked so hard on it," said Mum.

"It's not that."

"What then? Is it your exam results?"

"Maureen," Dad said warningly. Mum pursed up her lips.

"What about them?" I looked quickly from Mum to Dad.

"Dad and I weren't going to bring it up until after this gathering because we know how important it is to you. But the school rang. You passed, but your scholarship seems to be in jeopardy."

"Oh," I said, dully.

"Now, Maureen, we decided to leave all this until Monday," said Dad.

"Well, yes, but she may as well know we have a meeting at the school to discuss it. And, this party, sorry, *gathering*, seems to be a lot of the problem and now she doesn't even want to go." Mum sat down at the kitchen table for one of her zombie-inducing talks. "I just want to understand? Where are you going?"

"To my room," I said. How could I explain things to her when I didn't even understand them myself?

But once I was in there it felt more like a prison than a bedroom. I slid down the side of my bed to sit on the floor with my chin resting on my knees. I imagined Emma and Lindsay hanging out at Natasha's place all day, working on their self-tans and nails and getting excited together before pushing through the hedge to help Hugh and Sam decorate the party, and my eyes filled with tears of self-pity. I thought about them dancing to the playlists we'd downloaded, Natasha and I. I'd listened to about a billion songs searching for the right ones. I'd spent ages on it. Each song was to go with a particular scene like the soundtrack to a movie. I had all bases covered: *Smells Like Teen Spirit* by Nirvana, *Firework* by Katy Perry for girl dancing, *Can't Hold Us* by Macklemore, *Love Story* by Taylor Swift for dancing with boys, *Teenage Love Affair* by Alicia Keys for, well …

Would Sam notice if I wasn't there? Even though I wasn't planning to sleep with him at the party, I wouldn't mind if he did miss me. I hadn't seen him since the night of the dinner dance when he had shouldered past us in our dresses and our next scheduled practice for the debate wasn't until the following week. I had glimpsed him from a distance at the station on Tuesday, or so I thought. As I had lifted my arm in greeting, he disappeared as if he'd never been there at all.

Was he ignoring me or was I just being paranoid? All I knew was that I missed him. It felt like days and weeks later but after probably only a few hours, I got up and plucked my new eye pencil from my dresser. Natasha had one just like it and I had watched her apply it with bold strokes, amazed that she hadn't poked her eye out. If I raised an eyeliner pencil anywhere near my face, my eyes began to water and my eyelids fluttered. I gritted my teeth and applied it now to the rim of each lid. The effect was instant. Natasha was right; my eyes did look twice as big with make-up. I then experimented with a lipliner and blusher and rummaged in my dresser drawer for my hoop earrings and, in an act of defiance, my pendant. I pulled on a blue tank and a gathered white skirt. There I was, ready for a party I wasn't even going to. I stuck out my tongue at my reflection, put my pyjamas back on and dragged myself to the kitchen where I sheepishly apologised to Mum and Dad. They told me they loved me and together we'd work out what to do about the scholarship. I said I loved them, too, that something had come over me, and I had done some stupid things, but it was over now. From next Monday, everything would be different. I'd be different. They'd see.

"So, you're not going to the party?" Mum said, eyeing my pyjamas.

"Nope," and I told her about how Natasha had just been using me to get better marks and that she hadn't invited me to stay at her place or go over early to help.

"She doesn't sound like much of a friend. But she's not the one having the party, is she?" Dad said.

"Well, no. It's at Sam and Hugh's place."

"So, it's their gathering?"

"Sort of," I said.

"Well, then, they might need your help."

"Yes, I think you should go to this party," agreed Mum.

When I got there and stood alone on the driveway facing the lit-up house and listening to the throbbing bass of a party in full swing I almost turned around and went home again. But I didn't. I touched my dolphin pendant for luck and stepped slowly through the front door that had been propped open with a case of beer. Two guys pushed past me, "Yeehaw", coming out and I heard them crash land into the letterbox, splintering it. "Someone's gonna kill us for that," and the boys flopped back on the grass, dazed from the knock.

Inside, a couple was kissing against the wall and I nearly missed my step down into the lounge room. "Get a room," I heard someone say. Practically the entire Northcote Grammar population was inside. It was a mosh pit. Above them the ceiling fan fluttered with pink streamers, put up there by Natasha on Hugh's shoulders, I heard later. A group of guys stood underneath, downing tins of beer from holes in the side instead of through the top.

One of the guys saw me looking at him. "Want one?"

"What is it?" I asked.

"A shotgun."

"A what?"

"You punch a hole in the side of the can, take it to your mouth and then pop open the top. The air pressure sends the whole can of beer down your throat. It's the quickest way to get drunk." The guy burped and threw his empty can onto the glass coffee table.

"Charming offer," I said. "But no thanks."

A skinny little guy with a rat's tail shook up a bottle of sparkling wine – or was it cider? – and popped the cork. A stream of froth hit the wall and the group leaning against it. All this excess was vaguely shocking and nauseating. But I guess you didn't go to an open house party for meaningful conversation. All everybody there seemed to want to do was drink and hook up or break stuff. Poor Sam. I went to find him. I didn't have to go far. He was in the lounge room trying to get control of things.

"You're an animal – do you know that Fletcher?" he said. He picked up cans and bottles and shoved them into a garbage bag. He had a tight look on his face. It was good to see him even if it was the worst party of his life. I went up to him.

"Hey."

"Hey. I was starting to think you weren't coming."

"Um, well, I nearly didn't."

I saw Sam wince. I put my hand on his arm.

"I didn't mean it that way. It's just that I've had a big fight with my parents over flunking school and Natasha's not speaking to me."

"At least you came," he said. He reached forward and I thought for a second that he was going to, I don't know, touch my cheek or something, but he pulled an empty chip packet from the wall clock behind my head. He stuffed it in the garbage bag. "A friend of yours was looking for you earlier."

"Natasha?" I said, calmly. "Where is she?" I wanted to talk to her. I didn't know what I was going to say yet, but it was time to set her straight.

"Nope, I think her name was Brigitte. Tall, with hazel eyes. Good looking."

Huh? Sam didn't like Brigitte, did he? I felt something shift deep inside.

"I didn't know she was invited." I tried to sound casual. "She's more of a slumber party and campfire kind of girl."

Sam glanced grimly around the wreck that was his living room. "She was one of the few actually invited. My friend Flynn invited her. They swim together. But you probably already know that."

I didn't.

We watched a guy clamber up onto the furniture to play air guitar.

"I don't even know this guy." Sam called over to him, "Hey, would you do that on your own couch?

No? I didn't think so." He shook his head. "I could kill Toby. He was the one going around the school telling everybody about the party. It's not even his house. What a tosser." I didn't know if he referred to Toby or the air guitarist.

"It was on Facebook, you know," I said.

Sam stopped his garbage collecting. "Shit. Was it? Who put it up there?"

Should I tell him? Maybe later. I broke eye contact and gathered up some empty cans. "Let me help you." I threw them into the bag. "Umm, why isn't Hugh helping?"

"Good question. Too busy getting hot and heavy with Natasha somewhere, I suppose." Sam saw a guy open a can and spray it around the place. "Hey. Stop that," and he began to wade through a sea of legs in skinny jeans propped up on the coffee table and hollering, "Hey, Connor, put down the lamp, it's not a weapon." Over his shoulder, he said: "Go look for your friend. I'll find you later. Animals," I heard him mutter behind me. "People have to eat off that table."

Chapter 29

There was another tangled mess of shadowy figures talking in low voices in the pool room. It stank of sweat and dope and fruity perfume. A low square light just like the ones in the RSL club pool room lit up the centre of the table and the glossy balls as they spread out.

I saw Nick Hall, a can of beer in his hand and a cigarette or a joint dangling from his mouth, playing up to a group of girls in denim skirts. I wondered where Racquel was. My eyes slid past him to a familiar blonde head fixing drinks at the bar beyond. I forced my way through the players and onlookers to stand in front of her.

"Hi."

Natasha lifted her eyes. "Are you ready for the night of your life?"

I saw that her pupils were enormous orbs and she was slurring her words. What was she on?

"I need to talk to you," I began, then stopped when I saw the colour of the drinks. They were the exact shade of Masterfoods Hot English Mustard. "What are you doing?"

"Mixing very special cocktails." She didn't ask me why I was late. She stirred the drinks with her index finger. "Want one?"

"Nah huh."

No way I was going to end up the way I had during the Truth and Dare night.

"Sure?" She pushed one towards me. "They're selling like hotcakes."

She picked hers up. "Here's to us," downed it and turned to stare at the pool players. I turned, too, and side by side, almost companionably, we watched the game.

"Can I ask you a question?" I said, still not looking at her. "Did you throw out the necklace I gave you?" I felt Natasha's narrow shoulders lift up in a shrug.

"Why? I just want to know."

She set down the empty glass and pushed away from the bar. "Let's dance," and without waiting led me through the party saying, "Excuse me, excuse me, pardon me, coming through," until we were in the middle of the sticky floor. She stood there, moving just her hips to the music. I didn't even try to dance. There was no point. But it was right then and there, on the sticky dance floor, that I knew for certain. Natasha wasn't really my friend. I don't even think she liked me much. She had used me to get better grades and, maybe, to feel better about herself. Didn't they make a movie about girls like me? The friend who make the other girls look even better.

"Well, I don't care. I'm moving on." I said the words but Natasha was someplace else, eyes closed, and I don't think she even heard me. I looked away, disgusted with her and with myself.

I spied Hugh. He was wearing a white shirt, sleeves rolled up, out and not quite fully buttoned over a pair of jeans. He was leaning against the wall. I waved at him before I realised he was not alone and when I saw who was blowing in his ear, I drew in my breath sharply. Lindsay. I glanced quickly at Natasha. She was still slow-dancing by herself with her eyes closed. I swung back to Hugh and Lindsay. I thought of a saying of Aunt Gert's, 'Birds of a feather flock together'. I didn't understand what it meant before, but tonight as I watched my so-called friends implode, I finally figured it out. I also knew that I no longer wanted to be part of it – of them.

I pushed my way over to them. "Have you seen Brigitte?"

"Who?"

"Never mind. Where's Sam? Tell me, you're not going to ask who he is, too?"

Hugh just looked at me. I thought of Sam, picking up all the rubbish and trying to keep the guys from destroying the house and it made me feel like exploding.

"You might not care what happens to your house, but Sam does."

Hugh just kept looking at me as if I was crazy.

"Hey, what's your problem?" Lindsay said. "Why don't you chill. It's a party." Lindsay leaned into Hugh to kiss him on his cheek. "A very good party."

I turned on my heel and stalked off, fuming.

"What was that all about?" said Emma. She had come across from the other side of the room. Her lipstick was smudged and her water bottle was nearly empty.

"Look at them, would you. Who would do that to their best friend? I mean, come on."

"Yeah, what a bitch," said Emma. She ceremoniously held up her bottle. "Here's to a good time. Want some?"

The container was the temperature of urine in my hand. I suspiciously sniffed the neck. "That's not water, is it?"

She grinned. "Nope."

I gave it back to her. She leaned back to drain the last of the vodka. Lost her balance and tried to steady herself on the arm of a guys standing in the next group. The guy shoved her off. He was with two other guys and a girl who I recognised from school but two years ahead.

"Hey," I said. "Don't do that."

"Then control your friend," said the guy. The others laughed.

"C'mon, let's go," I said to Emma.

She swayed into me. "You're okay," and gave me a sloppy hug. I dragged her to the pool room and we watched a group playing pool. Among them was Toby. His freckled face lit up when he saw us and he came across and picked me up in a hug. "You made it," putting me down to eye off Emma. "Who's your friend?"

Emma finger waved him. "Hi, I'm Emma."

He picked her up in a hug even though they'd just met. Emma squealed.

"I'm picking up all the girls."

"Oh, come off it." I couldn't help but smile. "Are those lines really working for you?"

He see-sawed his hand, still grinning. "So-so."

He had on a T-shirt that said *Make Love, Not War* and his hair was dishevelled like he'd just awoken from hibernation.

"How about this?" He jerked his head to indicate he meant the party, raising a fist in a gesture of victory when he caught the eye of a couple of guys. He peered at me. "You don't look like you're having fun. Aren't you having fun? She is." He pointed to Emma. "You're having fun, aren't you?"

Emma gave him a shoulder shimmy and giggled. "Sure."

"Good. It's my party. Everybody's gotta have fun at my party."

"Isn't it Sam and Hugh's party?"

"Theirs, too."

"Then you should be helping."

"I am. Guest relations." His mouth twitched.

"Is that what you call it?"

"Yeah. Wanna play pool?"

Emma clapped her hands. "Love to play. I gotta warn you, I'm a terrible player." She mimed taking a wobbly shot to prove her point, nearly taking out her own eye.

"Steady there." Toby put his arm around her waist. "Don't worry. I'll teach you. It's easy."

Emma tittered. "Lead me to the pool table."

What was it with girls and vodka? It was like they used alcohol to say and do all the things they'd longed to when sober but didn't have the guts. Me, I didn't think inhibitions were such a bad thing.

Toby winked at me over his shoulder. "Coming, Lucy?"

"Nah." I said. "You go ahead, though."

"Come on, Lucy." Emma beseeched me. "It'll be fun."

"I want to find my friend Brigitte."

"Just one game. Then we'll help you find your friend." Toby leaned back to snake the arm not already around Emma around my waist and I found myself being dragged along with them.

"A quick game, then," I said.

It turned out we were playing with Nick and Toby.

"You play with Nick." Toby began to rack up. "I'll take Emma here. Teach her some 'Tobe' moves." Oh, puleeze.

I turned to Nick, smiled super sweetly. "Where's Racquel?"

He had the decency to look sheepish. "Er, at a family thing. So, are you any good at pool?"

"Nope," I said. But that was a fib. I messed up most ball sports, but thanks to three years living near a bunch of miners with access to their recreational room, I was a bit of a pool shark. I'm going to enjoy this, I thought.

Emma couldn't take her eyes off Nick. She nudged me to whisper, "Isn't that Nick Hall, the guy who took you to the dinner dance instead of Lindsay?"

"Shush." I glanced over at Toby and Nick. But they were busy setting up balls and hadn't heard.

Nick handed me a pool cue. "Do you want me to chalk your tip?"

The way he said it made me think he was talking about something else entirely. He really couldn't help himself, could he? Then I realized that he wasn't even looking at me. Through the doorway, he was watching Natasha out there on the dance floor.

I expected to feel more – pain or something. I mean, for a while there, Nick Hall was all I could think about. In my dreams we were married with two kids. But I felt nothing. Huh, how about that? Was it just me or were all girls this fickle?

Toby made a big show of chalking up and spouting the rules like he was the expert. He lined up his shot, legs spread and left eye closed, lifted his head slightly, told some guy opposite to get out of the way, then sent the ball straight into a pocket without hitting another ball first.

"Shot," said Nick, dryly.

"Wasn't my fault. Anderson over there put me off. Anderson, would you piss off."

It was Nick's turn and casually he balanced the end of his stick on two fingers and smoothly fired off his shot. He turned his head and fired again. Five seconds and two balls sunk. Did he practise being cool in his sleep?

"Way to go." Toby clapped Nick on the shoulder and made him miss his third shot.

"Dumb fuck," said Nick, lightly and he flicked Toby's forehead.

"Ow," said Toby, rubbing his head. Natasha had drifted over by now, still half-swaying to the music. "Will I kiss it better for you?" she asked softly.

"Better not. Hugh'd have my nuts," said Toby, looking disappointed all the same.

"Can I play?" she drifted around him, a will of the wisp with a piece of hair in her mouth and her eyes large and seeing a horizon no one else could see. Was she totally wasted?

"Yep. Here's the stick. You're up next," said Nick. His smile had widened as he watched and waited like a lion about to pounce.

"Is this how you hold it?" Natasha asked, looking up at him.

"No, here let me show you." Nick put his arms around her and leaned her into the table. With his hand over hers, she aimed and shot. The balls slowly spread out. Not one made it as far as the edge.

"Gotta hit it a little harder, but good try," said Toby, rubbing his hands nervously as if he could see this exploding in his face.

It was Emma's turn, but the effort of holding herself upright was more than she could handle. She leaned against the wood panelled wall. Natasha scooped up Nick's pack of cigarettes from the edge of the table and leaned next to Emma, who tried to rest her head on Natasha's shoulder. Natasha jiggled it off. Emma moaned and tried to get comfortable, still standing, with her head tipped back. Natasha lit up a cigarette, with considerable care, and blew smoke out, watching it intently as it dissipated in tufts. She picked a stray bit of tobacco from her lower lip.

"Here: you'd better have her go," said Toby, giving up on Emma. He handed me the cue.

This was my chance, and I took it. Without a word, I stepped up to the table. I blew my fringe casually out of my eyes and proceed to sink all the balls, one by one. Nick and Toby watched in silence.

"Want another game?" I said, passing my cue to Nick. It was my turn to wink and I smirked, too, when I saw the looks on their faces. "You can close your mouths now."

"Impressive," said Toby.

"What's my prize?" I beamed at them.

Toby and Nick looked at each other and back at me in a sort of leer.

I put my hands on my hips and rolled my eyes, "Not that kind of prize." Hey, this flirting thing wasn't so hard.

Toby raised his eyes at Nick. "Best of three?"

I attempted a sidelong look through my lashes and caught sight of Sam. He was watching, a couple of empties in his hands, and suddenly I didn't feel nearly so sexy or clever.

"Nah, I'm going to find Brigitte and help Sam tidy up. Coming, Emma?"

Emma opened her mouth to answer and vomited all over her sneakers instead. I managed to jump clear of the splash. Natasha wasn't so fortunate and some of the spew caught in the cuff of her jeans and dripped off onto her wedges.

"Gross." Nick and Toby backed away.

Natasha's lovely face puckered and she shook her foot trying to dislodge the vomit. "Get it off me," she shrieked. I searched for something to wipe her down with. All I could get my hands on was a discarded denim jacket. Was it Toby's? Nick's? I couldn't remember. I hesitated. No way. I couldn't use someone's jacket. But Natasha snatched it from me and wiped herself down. "It stinks. I've got to wash this off. Lucy, help me," and she stomped off expecting me to be right behind her.

Chapter 30

A week ago, I would have followed Natasha to the ends of the earth, but tonight I didn't even want to go to the bathroom with her. So I didn't. I stayed behind to clean up Emma. I was free. The thought was exhilarating.

I was sick of trying to please a girl who wasn't easily pleased and who, most of the time, wasn't very nice, either. I'd finally realised that she didn't seem to like me much no matter how I tried to change, twist myself into knots to maintain her high standards of how a popular girl should look and behave. I was who I was: small, intense, with principles. It was as simple and as complicated as that.

So I would stay and help Emma even though I knew she wasn't much of a friend, either. I couldn't leave Emma passed out in her own vomit. That would be wrong. What if she choked to death? They taught us about that during first aid lessons. Then I would look for my friend Brigitte.

Emma didn't help herself, though, lolling about like a great walrus. Eventually, I got her away from the vomit and let her slide down into a raggedy doll posture to study what I would do about the pile of sick. How the hell was I going to clean it up? I spied a half-empty long-neck on the window sill and picked it up. Would that do it?

"You're looking at the wrong tool for the job." It was Sam and he was holding up a plastic cup.

"See?" He knelt beside me and started to scoop.

"What?" he said catching my amazement. "I was a Cub Scout."

"I don't feel very well." Emma moaned and moved her head from side to side.

"Funny that," said Sam.

"Are you going to be sick again?" I said, poised to jump out of her way.

"No. Yes." She doubled over, a dribble of spit dangled from her mouth. She wiped it with the back of her hand and then started moaning again.

"I really wish she'd stop that," I said.

"How's she getting home?" asked Sam.

"I think she's staying at Natasha's."

"I don't think she could even get herself to the next room; girl's paralytic."

"We can't leave her here."

"We can't take her to a bedroom. What if she throws up all over the sheets?" So, we dragged her by the shoulders to a dusty corner of the games room. She was a dead weight and her hair trailed behind her in a matted tangle.

"Are you putting her into the recovery position?" Sam watched me roll the unconscious girl onto her side, pull up her top knee and spread out her arms. "Nice one."

"Thanks. I was a Girl Guide." I sat back on my heels to examine my work. "Will she be okay here? Should I call Mr Fielding?"

"Nope. So, do you like him?"

"Who? Mr Fielding?" I continued to survey the prone girl.

"No. Nick."

I looked in surprise into eyes that were tonight mostly pewter grey. "Why would you think that?"

Sam shrugged. "Because I saw you both together tonight. Because you went to the dinner dance with him."

"I don't like Nick Hall," I said firmly.

"Forget it," said Sam, shaking his head slightly. "I gotta get rid of this rubbish. Coming?"

"Ohh, this night is getting better and better. I couldn't possibly refuse such an exciting offer," and then, when I saw his face, "I'm kidding."

The aluminium cans were stacked in a row around the side of the house.

"It's a great party. I reckon everyone here, except, maybe, Emma, would give it a 10. Toby'd give it an 11," I said as we picked our way over the paving stones, some of them cracked.

Sam grunted. "He would. The douche can't count." I skipped over a jagged crack.

"What are you doing?" he said.

"Can't touch the lines. Didn't you ever play that game as a kid?"

Sam pushed the garbage bag into the bin and returned the red plastic lid with a clatter that echoed through the darkness. He wiped his hands on the grass at his feet.

The low-slung moon cast stumpy shadows on the wall. I made the shape of a wolf with my hand, then a rabbit.

"Can we stay here for a while? I've been so busy, cleaning up vomit and de-friending Natasha. I need to rest," I said.

We sank down, resting our backs against the still-warm bricks of the wall, our eyes closed. Sam's knees were bent. I sat cross-legged, tucking in my white skirt over the triangle of my legs.

"I thought you and Natasha were best friends."

"Not any more. We sort of had a falling out," I said.

"Since when?" Sam made himself more comfortable.

"Since tonight."

"Was it because you helped Emma?"

"Actually, I think it happened before tonight. It turns out that we mightn't have ever been friends."

Sam made a noise.

"Did you just snort?" I said, wondering if I was right in thinking that Sam didn't think too much of Natasha. "She's your brother's girlfriend. One time I thought you liked her too."

"She's not my type. I admit she's gorgeous. But only on the outside."

I sat up straight. This was interesting. "Meaning?"

"Her looks are only skin deep. Underneath, she's pretty ugly. Like how she made you go to the dinner dance with Nick."

"I wanted to go. It was fun."

"I just think she needs to control everyone around her and she uses people to get what she wants. She used you."

"I kinda figured that. But you know what? I was sort of using her, too, so I guess that makes us even."

"What were you using her for?" Sam sounded surprised.

I chewed my lip: would I tell him?

"To be popular."

Sam was silent.

"Yeah, I know, pretty sad and desperate of me."

"Why would you think being friends with Natasha would make you more popular?" He sounded confused, like he really didn't get it. "You're way better than her."

I laughed until I realised he was actually being serious.

"But she's so gorgeous. You've said so. Your brother thinks so."

"But that's not enough. Anyway, he doesn't know what she gets up to behind his back."

I moved around to look at him properly. "What are you talking about?"

"Don't tell me you don't know?"

"I don't. I really don't," I said.

"She sleeps around." He looked away like he was embarrassed to have to tell me. I was about to deny it, but when I thought back to the night of the dinner dance and the lift we got to the oval, I realised that it was true. I already knew.

"Just tonight when I was cleaning up I found her fooling around with Nick Hall in the garage."

"No way. But he has a girlfriend." And he was flirting with *me*.

"He doesn't care about Racquel. I feel sorry for her. He's made her crazy."

"Does Hugh know?"

"Dunno. Do you think I should tell him?"

I recalled his taut face watching Natasha all by herself on the dance floor and thought that maybe he already knew. Sam leaned his head on the wall and closed his eyes. I closed mine. Even though we were around the side, I could still hear the party, the laughing, the throb of the music, the clink of bottles. I wondered if it was shaping up as the party of the century like Natasha had hoped.

"Sam?"

"Hmmm."

"What are you thinking about?"

"I'm thinking about kissing you."

My eyes flew open and I turned my face. There he was, close, his grey-green eyes dark and luminous with wanting. He leaned forward and his lips touched mine gently, tentatively. Before I knew it, my arms were around his neck and I was kissing him back. He gave a sort of groan and began to kiss me harder until I wanted to explode. "Oh, hell," he said, pulling away and pushing his hands through his hair. His eyes took me in. I was sure he could see right through me, to my liquid insides. He groaned again. "I've gotta stop for a sec." But my mouth sought his out again. I didn't want him to stop.

"I mean it, Lucy. Or I won't be able to." He sat back with his knees up and his arms wrapped around them. I realised then and there that I was in love; that I had been falling in love with him slowly these past weeks and I didn't even know it, even when Natasha was telling me to sleep with him. The thought gave me goosebumps. I remembered the stab of pain I'd felt when he'd commented on Brigitte's appearance. It was jealousy, pure and simple.

I leaned back, too, a little shaky.

"Wow," I said. "I didn't see that coming."

"You're kidding? You didn't know I liked you?"

I shook my head. "I had no idea."

"For a clever person, you aren't too bright sometimes. I've liked you since the first time I saw you on the tennis courts. Hugh saw it right away."

"Really? I thought it was Natasha you couldn't take your eyes off."

"It was a bit hard not to, the way she was flaunting it."

I thought about Natasha and how she'd licked her lips after drinking from the bubbler that afternoon on the tennis court. Natasha needed to be desired. It only just came to me, but I knew it to be true. She was addicted to it. It filled her up in all the places she was empty. A shrink – or my mother – might say it was all because her mother had abandoned her. All I knew was without her fan club Natasha was nothing; a nobody. When she was desired, she had all the power. She was alive. She was not invisible. This was a girl I didn't understand. Then again, maybe I did. I didn't want to be invisible either.

"Paul reckoned she came on to him once." I tried to focus on what Sam was saying.

"Who? Paul?" It was my turn to snort.

"What does that mean?"

"He's a pig," I said, but stopped right there. Paul was Sam's friend, after all.

"Well, anyway. I just saw him. He's got his eye on your friend, Brigitte. I'd better warn Flynn tonight, next time I see him."

My hand went to my mouth. What if he tried it on with her like he did with me in the weights room? Shit. I had been looking for Brigitte before the pool game – before flirting with Nick, cleaning up Emma and kissing Sam – for no particular reason except perhaps to say how sorry I was for being such a crappy friend and that I wanted to be her friend again. Now I had to find her because I was worried. I moved to get up. "I want to look for Brigitte."

"Okey dokey." Sam stood and held out his hand to help me up. He was a lean shadow in his black jeans and black T-shirt. His smile was goofy, but he still looked pretty cute and when he took a long time to let go of my hand, my heart thumped against my ribs, like a budgie fluttering around in a cage, and I very nearly forgot all about Brigitte all over again.

"Your hand's sticky," I said, trying to be normal.

"So is yours," he said, smiling. "Where do you want to try first?"

"The bedrooms." I didn't want to say it in case it was true so I whispered it.

Chapter 31

We held hands on the way back inside. Okay, it was a cheesy thing to do, but it felt comfortable and, honestly, I couldn't imagine my hand anywhere else. We stopped at a knot of people, none of whom I knew, in the darkened hall outside the bathroom. The door was closed and one of the group was banging on it. "Hurry up, wouldya?"

"What's going on?" I said, looking curiously at the unfamiliar faces staring back in the half-light.

"Some girls have locked themselves in and we've been waiting here for about half an hour."

"Why don't you use the toilet upstairs?" said Sam.

"Jeez. Have you seen that toilet? Someone has been sick all over the floor. It's disgusting, man."

"You didn't think to clean it up?" said Sam, through locked teeth.

The guy looked at him in amazement. "Why would I do that?" I had to squeeze Sam's hand very tightly then. The guy sensed hostility and looked more closely at him. "Don't I know you?"

"Hugh's brother," said Sam, tightly.

"Then do you think you could get the bloody door open. Some of us need to take a slash," he said.

"What's wrong with a tree out front? Better still, why don't you use the toilet at your place."

"Fuck off," said the same guy. He jerked his head at the girls of the group. "I'll use the tree. But what about them? They can't piss standing up." The girls acted like he'd just said the funniest thing in the world.

"They can use my parents' toilet – it's off their bedroom, first door on the right. But I'm warning you, if you mess it up, I'm gonna come looking for you." Sam pointed at the guy to show he wasn't fooling.

The group trooped off and we stared at the round brass door handle. I felt dread, but I didn't know why.

"Hey, are you coming out or not?" called Sam through the keyhole.

Just as I was about to give up, I heard a giggle and a voice say, "Give us a minute," and Lindsay and Natasha fell out, their eyes glazed and secretive. Natasha's smile grew even wider when she saw us together and she put herself between us, arms about our waists.

"Knew you would do it," she said, carefully pronouncing each word.

"What are you talking about?" said Sam.

"Ask Lucy," she said.

Sam stepped away from them, tipping his head a little to one side, sizing them up. "You've been having fun again, Natasha? Tell me, did you invite those guys with the tats?"

Natasha shrugged. "Why?"

"They're smashing up the house, that's why."

"It's a party. What do you expect?" said Natasha. "Lindsay, we're going to find someone else more fun to play with." She turned and walked away, trailing a languid arm along the wall as if to say, follow me.

"Charming," said Sam with sarcasm. "Let's keep looking."

We checked the whole house – the bedrooms, the kitchen, the garage and the living room and, for the millionth time, the games room. We were running out of places. While we were in the games room we paused to see how Emma was doing. She was snoring like a wino. Where was Brigitte? We were running out of places.

"She must have gone home," I said.

"We haven't tried outside," said Sam.

"Good idea. She could be in the pool," I said. "She's a swimmer."

I pulled back the sliding door and stepped out on to the patio. The music had died away and I figured it was pretty late by now. The murmur of voices, and every now and again, mellow laughter, floated up from figures stretched out on plastic lounges around the edge of the pool. A solitary beer bottle was standing on a Lilo in the middle of the pool. Pizzas must have been ordered (when?) An empty box had been frisbeed into the tree and a half eaten slice was floating just beneath the surface of the pool. How gross can you get? I tried to make out faces in the dim moonlight. A match was struck up. Then a cigarette glowed through the dark. I couldn't see who was smoking it, but I could guess.

Someone had taken off her dress, leaving it beside the pool, and was in the water performing handstands, walking under water with her bare legs sticking up like swizzle sticks in a cocktail. Was it Brigitte? I looked closely as the girl surfaced, the water streaming down her back. It was Natasha. So, she'd found something else to do. I wondered where Lindsay had got to.

"Come and get me," she said to the guy holding the cigarette, and splashed away. He flicked the butt into the garden and turned his face into the porch light. I tightened my grip on Sam's hand. It was Scott Morgan.

"Let's go," I said and pulled Sam away, beyond the light, further into the garden, past the giant oak and to a corner where the party became a tiny pinprick of white noise. A voice, faintly from the house, cried out, "Turn it up. Love this song."

"The neighbours are gonna start complaining," said Sam, glumly. All the fight had gone out of him. I patted his arm. "Hang in there."

We sat on a weathered slatted seat rough with tiny splinters that pulled threads in my skirt. I yanked my skirt free and it frothed all over Sam's denim knee. He put his arm around me and our shadows merged. That's when I heard it: a squeak rather like a wheelbarrow on the footpath. I stiffened in surprise and Sam froze.

"What? Did I do something wrong?"

"Sorry. It's just that I heard a noise behind us," I whispered.

"A possum? They sometimes sound weird." Sam whispered, too.

"Maybe," I said, doubtfully. "Listen."

We waited, our foreheads touching, in the dark. I heard the squeak again, and rustling; a low croon.

"That sounded human," said Sam.

"What should we do?"

"Probably go back to the party. We don't want to disturb anyone," said Sam. He made to get up.

"Please." It was a girl's voice. Something in its tone freaked me out.

I pinched Sam's arm. "Hear that?"

He nodded, pressed his finger to his lips. I scooped back my skirt and twisted around so that I was leaning over the back of the bench, trying to be as quiet as possible and peering through the shrubs to see if I could make out what was happening on the triangle of moss in the corner of the garden. That's when I saw them.

Brigitte was lying face up on the ground. Her hair was spread out behind her, her eyes squeezed tightly shut. Her lips were moving, but I couldn't hear what she was saying. Then a hand slid across her mouth. I saw, then, that her jeans were down around her ankles and her knees, bare round orbs, were being pushed apart. His other arm was raised high in the air and I could see the red light of a mobile phone set to record.

"You know you want it." Paul's voice was a growl and it brought me to my senses.

"Hey. What the hell do you think you're doing?" I surprised myself and Sam, too, because he jumped. My voice was loud and fierce. Sam got to his feet.

"Paul? Is that you?" he said. Paul's curly head lifted and he shifted slightly to rest on an elbow.

"Do you mind? We'd like some privacy here." He dropped his phone and withdrew his hand from between Brigitte's legs, and adjusted his clothes.

"Paul? Is that you?"

"Sam?"

"What's going on?"

"What do ya think? And we'd like to get back to it, if you don't mind."

I stared at Sam. I shook my head, just a little. Sam lifted his shoulders as if to say, what should we do?

I hated Paul's guts, he made my skin crawl. But maybe Brigitte didn't, maybe she wanted this. My stomach clenched again. Damn. I couldn't be sure. I took another look at Brigitte. She was still lying on Paul's denim jacket. Except for her jeans, she was mostly still dressed. How far had they got? Was this what she wanted? I didn't know. I wished she wouldn't lie there. I wished she'd get up. I wished she'd say something.

"Brigitte?" I moved closer. That was when I saw dirty streaks of revulsion on her pale face and I knew. She didn't want it. Not like this, anyway. I crouched beside her. She struggled to sit up and I rubbed her shivering back, feeling the coat hanger curve of her spine. She began to cry.

"Brigitte?" I said again.

But she couldn't speak. She could only cry.

I looked across her to Paul: "You did this," I said.

"Did what exactly?" said Paul, belligerently.

"You know," I said.

"We did precisely nothing."

"You had her pants down and were on top of her. You had your *phone*. That's not *nothing*," I said.

"What are you? Her mum?"

"Muum. I want my mum." Brigitte cried even harder.

"I'll ring her, don't worry. She'll come and get you," I said, soothingly.

"She's going to kill me. You can't tell her, Lucy. Promise me you won't tell her."

"I promise," I said.

"Tell her what, anyway?" said Paul. "*Nothing* happened."

"Then why is Brigitte crying her eyes out?" I stared at him.

"What were you doing, Paul?" Sam put the question mildly. Paul shook his head, "Stay outta this, mate."

"Can't do that," said Sam. Paul felt around the ground for his phone, pocketing it when he found it and making wind-up gestures with his hands. "Show's over. I'm going back to the party. Coming?" he said to Sam.

Sam shook his head. Paul pulled a face and started back.

I watched him leave. "He's gone now, Briggy. It's just us. You can tell us. Did he …?"

She pulled up the bottom of her T-shirt and used it to wipe her nose.

"No! At least, I don't think so." Brigitte took a deep breath. "I'm a bit confused."

"Take it slow," I said.

"Okay, I was in the kitchen talking to him and then we were out here." She touched the side of her head.

"Ow. That really hurts. Can you see anything there? Am I bleeding?"

"Nope." I touched her head. "I can feel a lump, though. Did you hit something?" She shook her head. "Fall over?"

"I can't remember." Brigitte's eyes widened and welled up and she buried her face in her hands. I stopped patting her and caught Sam's eye. He shuffled on his feet, looking sick and scared. I put up my hand to say don't spook her.

"Did Paul hit you?"

She didn't answer.

"What did he do?"

Brigitte's voice was muffled. "Don't hate me."

"Why would I hate you? We're friends."

"Are we?" Her complete lack of irony sliced through me.

She fumbled for the words. "Natasha Fielding had given me this drink and was being really nice asking about my swimming and stuff. Paul came over, chatting us up. Then Natasha left. And Paul said he wanted to go somewhere quiet. I couldn't find Flynn and I said I wanted to look for you. He said, fine: he knew exactly where you were. And I believed him." She stopped and wiped her eyes with the heel of her palm.

"Then we came out here. That's when he changed. It was horrible. He, he was rough … and he wouldn't listen when I told him to stop it. He, ah, pushed me to the ground and, and started, you know, pulling down my jeans, and, and ..." She trailed off with such a look of shame that that I shut my eyes for an instant.

When I looked up at Sam, he was shaking his head in disbelief – not with Brigitte's story but that Paul would do such a terrible thing. I did. I believed every filthy word she didn't say.

There was a movement to my left and Paul came out from behind the trunk of the oak.

"What are you doing back?" I said.

His eyes were sweeping the ground until he spied what he was looking for: his denim jacket. "Getting this. It's Tsubi." He yanked at the sleeve, tipping Brigitte off. Seeing her scrabbling about in the dirt seemed to please him. What a creep.

"It's bullshit, you know," he said noticing the look of disgust on my face. "What she's saying about me. Just not true. She was fully consenting to all of it."

Brigitte disappeared into herself. Sam stepped up to Paul. "Why are you saying all this?"

"Defending myself?" Paul still wanted to be in control of the situation. "Someone's got to." He grew wheedling, gave Sam a nudge. "She wanted it. They all do, man."

"She did *not*," I said. His attempt to shame Brigitte and show that Sam and he were on the same team and wanting the same things, was making me feel sicker than his denials. He was a misogynistic bastard.

I remembered how he had forced himself on me in the weights room, putting his thick tongue in my mouth and his hands all over me until I wanted to throw up.

Now. At this moment, I wanted to smash his face in.

He leered in Brigitte's direction. "Just ask *her*."

"I have," I said. I was trembling by then. I said: "You're an arsehole. You know that? You think you can treat girls like objects and get away with it. Well, you can't."

He looked me up and down like I was something dirty, then spat at the ground to the left of my feet; his way of telling me that I was just a dumb, stupid girl who was overreacting. And that did it.

A great wall of scarlet anger bled across my vision and I gathered myself up and shoved him as hard as I could. I put everything into it but it wasn't enough.

"Bitch," he said, shoving me right back. I fell hard onto the ground, winded. There was roaring in my ears but righteous anger and adrenaline put me straight back on my feet. I was still powerful.

"Bastard."

"Slut."

"Rapist!"

Paul made a fist and wound it back to punch me. Sam grabbed his arm from behind. "You don't hit girls." His voice was low, angry, but still in control. Paul wrenched his arm free, his hand still up and ready to deck me, anything to shut me up.

"Leave her alone," said Sam.

"Yeah?" said Paul, slyly. "She didn't want me to leave her alone before."

Sam ignored the comment. Paul kept at it.

"Why don't you tell him, Lucy?"

I glared at him. I couldn't believe this.

"You wanted me to give it to you tonight, too." Paul gave a taunting sneer. "I saw my name on your list."

"Shut up," said Sam. "Shut the fuck up or I'm going to bloody kill you."

"Fuck you, Curtis."

The distance between them had closed to almost nothing, just a sliver of air. They were nose to nose, chest to chest, hearts pumping, eyeballing one another. Shove. Shove. The shoving took them back towards the party. I held my breath.

Chapter 32

Who threw the first punch? I will never be 100 per cent sure. One minute Paul and Sam were facing off, the next Sam was bent double, sawing in air, and Paul was holding the bridge of a bloody nose.

"That hurt," he said. I put up my hands so I couldn't see anything. All I could hear was music from the party – OneRepublic, of all things – and Brigitte's chattering teeth.

Then everything went silent and I found myself watching two boys fight. It gave me a peculiar sense of remoteness – of being in a dream, of nothing being quite real or involving me.

I was wrong about that. It had everything to do with me. I'd never felt more sickened and ashamed in my life. How could I have been such a fool? This has gone too far. Stop. But the word got caught between my chest and throat.

I had become invisible by then, anyway. The two boys were long gone, into the dark, desperate place that boys go when they have something to prove or someone to save. All I could do was to wait.

With small predator eyes, hard and bright, Paul lunged at Sam. He had Sam by the windpipe and squeezed hard. Sam's face went crimson under the pressure until his thrashing elbow jabbed Paul's guts and he loosened his grip. Then Paul jumped on top of Sam and together they rolled on the ground until they lost momentum. They lay on the pathway alongside the pool, panting. Quickly Paul manoeuvred himself so that Sam was pinned between his thighs and Paul was half-sitting on him. My hands went back up to cover my eyes the way I watched horror films, seeing everything from between my fingers.

Flattened oak leaves had collected on the back of Paul's denim jacket and they fell off, one by one, each time he slugged at Sam. Any second now, someone was going to come over and help Sam. If only I could move … I became aware of Brigitte sobbing beside me. It unfroze me.

"Come on," I said pulling Brigitte along with me. "We've got to find Hugh."

There he was, tall and straight on the dark square lawn on the other side of the pool. He hadn't seen the fight.

"You've gotta help Sam. Paul is killing him."

"What do you mean?"

"Just come with me."

By the time we reached them, Sam was practically unconscious. Hugh cursed and called Paul every name he could think of as he took him by the neck and shook him until his teeth rattled. Finally, he punched him and Paul fell back. Hugh dropped to his knees beside Sam, who groaned through his pulpy face and tried to get away.

"It's me, Sammy. Don't move," he said, trying to mop up some of the blood with the edge of his shirt. "Shit. Shit, you're a mess."

Paul's fist came out of the darkness like a freight train and caught Hugh on the side of his head. Hugh nearly went over. But something, probably the adrenaline maxing out in his veins, brought him to his feet, his hand already in a fist which he rammed into Paul's mouth. The force of it busted open Hugh's knuckles and sent Paul flying through the air, twisted and thrashing, all the way to the knife edge of the pool. He went down, hard and fast, and didn't get up. A puddle of blood, the colour of sticky cough syrup, spread out from beneath his body and across the pebblecrete. It was weird, but I felt the air pressure drop, and I knew in that instant that everything had changed forever.

Brigitte started to scream then, and wouldn't stop. "Shut *up*," I said covering my ears until she fell silent.

Finally, I could move. I crawled to where Sam lay in the shadow of the pool. He tried to get up, fell back, slippery with blood. I didn't dare, couldn't bear, to look at his face so I fixed my eyes on his pale white hand. I took it: it was warm and I nearly dropped it. I expected it to be cold. What could I say to make him feel better?

"It's okay," I said, unaware that I was only two feet away from the dying boy. The hem of my skirt was soaking up the blood like litmus paper, and nothing would ever be okay again. When I stood up, I saw that my knees were cut and bleeding. There was so much blood. It was everywhere.

I wished I could say in my statement I'd done something useful, then, like calling an ambulance or the cops, or fixing Sam up but I was a hopeless case. All I could do was cry, so hard snot ran out, and say over and over: "There's blood on my dress. My mum's going to kill me." I suppose, like everyone, I was in shock.

For some reason, though, I had a clear picture of Mr Fielding looming out of the darkness of next door, incongruous in his velour navy striped dressing gown that stopped at his thigh, yelling: "Do you know what time it is?" until he caught sight of the broken door, the crying girls and all that blood.

"Where's my daughter?" he roared. He must have called for an ambulance because not long after that, I heard through the buzz in my ears the wail of sirens, coming closer, closer. Then eerie hollow silence until the police walked through, shaking their heads. The first lot of paramedics worked on Sam. A second pair arrived and took away Paul.

Eventually, only Hugh, Toby, Natasha and I were left waiting to talk to police. Natasha stood beside Mr Fielding, in the middle of the lawn, fully clothed, mouth and eyes dry. The only hint of her earlier behaviour were the wet marks of her underwear and drooping eyelids. I heard Mr Fielding ask if he could take her home, pointing next door. I'd never forget the sight of her trailing home behind her dad; her hair a damp tangled mess down her back and her bare feet looking like a modern-day Daisy Buchanan.

I waited until it was my turn to speak to a policeman. "Will he be okay?" I said. The policeman looked at me strangely. Was I under the influence, too, like most of the partygoers? "No. He's deceased."

I had meant Sam, of course, who had been seen to by one of the medics, his left eye nearly closed and his face all cut up and swollen, before being taken to North Shore Hospital, but I didn't say so. I was ashamed that I hadn't given a second thought to Paul.

"You'll have to give a statement down at the station tomorrow, but I'd like to ask you a few questions now." I nodded, my mind still with Sam.

"Do you know how the fight started?" he asked, pencil stabbing at a small notepad with metal binding. Clumps of grey hair sprouted from his ears and beetled across his brow and he'd missed a bit on his chin when shaving.

I couldn't speak.

"We think there were about 100 youths at this party. That father over there said you'd invited most of them."

Me? But I still didn't say a word.

"Where were you when the fight occurred? Did you see what happened to the deceased?"

He was getting impatient. I wished he'd stop referring to Paul as the deceased. It sounded so final. And, I suppose it was: death.

"Well, do you know the other two boys involved?"

I pictured Hugh and how he had gone to pieces in front of everyone when he realised Paul was dead and he'd killed him and was probably going to be charged with murder. How the ambos then had to sedate him and half carry him across the patio and through the gaping hole that once were sliding doors. I thought about Paul and what he'd done to Brigitte. And Sam and our kiss and how firmly his hand had gripped mine while we were looking for her.

"The guy over there," I said, finally, pointing. "He's the brother of the guy who went to hospital. Sam. He's my friend."

Amid the chaos and horror and shame, I clung to that. It was, after all, true. As it turned out, he was about the only one I had.

* * *

I made Mum drive past Natasha's house on the way home from giving my statement to the police the following day, a Sunday. Sunday Bloody Sunday. I don't quite know why. I suppose I wanted to see her. Make sure that she was as sorry for everything as I was. Mum waited in the car while I got out. I stood on the edge of the gutter, staring at her house. I wanted to go up to the door, knock, go in but I couldn't move from where I was. A movement in the window caught my eye. It was Natasha. She stared at me for a minute. I looked at her face, her beautiful hard face and I knew that she regretted none of it, was sorry for none of it. She felt nothing.

Natasha didn't return to school the following Monday, nor the next. In fact, she stayed away for the rest of the term. There were only a few days remaining anyway. I rang her to see how she was and Mr Fielding curtly told me that she was busy. She didn't return my calls and I heard in a roundabout way that she'd been sent to a hospital in Melbourne. Someone thought it was to treat anorexia. Another girl heard that she was having a baby.

I never saw her again. And if you want to know the truth, by then I didn't care.

Chapter 33

I guess you could say I grew up a lot the night of the party. I wish it had never happened. But it had and what was done was done and I had to face up to my part in it and deal with it. And, anyway, as my mum would say: sorry doesn't always cut it.

She was right, but the least I could do was try. So, one fine Saturday morning I went into the dewy garden with Mum's secateurs and gathered up as many flowers as I could find. I wrapped them in tissue paper, wound one of Milly's ballet ribbons tightly around them and went over to Brigitte's house.

"Hi, Mrs Riley. Is Brigitte home?"

Hello, Lucy. How are you feeling?"

"Fine, thanks," I said because telling a parent anything else would have been dangerous.

"Brigitte's in her room. Go on through."

Her door was open, and I could see her lying on her bed, her legs dangling over the end, reading, but I knocked anyway and waited until she twisted around to rest on her shoulder.

"Oh, hi, Lucy," she said, blinking. "What are you doing here?"

"Hi, Briggy," I said. "These are for you," and I held out the posy. She didn't do anything straightaway. She just looked at the flowers in my hand.

"Thanks," she said, eventually. "Are they from your mum's garden?"

"I picked them this morning. Can I sit down?"

She waved me onto the bed and I sat on the edge, still holding the flowers. She sat up after a minute, took the posy and put it in the glass of water by her bedside.

"They look nice," I said, and bit my lip. This was hard.

"Briggy?" I took a big breath, "I'm sorry. About everything."

Brigitte played with the tassles on her bedspread. "That's okay," she said in a low voice, "Well, sort of. I mean, Paul's not okay. But that's not your fault. You were just helping me. If anything it's mine for letting him ... do that ..."

"None of it was your fault," I said fiercely. "He sexually assaulted you."

"He didn't rape me, though. You and Sam stopped him." Brigitte still spoke to the bedspread. "I can't believe he's … dead."

I squeezed my eyes shut so I wouldn't see Paul's face in the bushes or the way his blood bloomed onto my skirt like it had been dipped into a bowlful of Condy's crystals.

"Is Sam all right?"

I didn't answer. The truth was I didn't know. When I had visited him in hospital with some of Mum's caramel slice, I had been shocked by what I saw. There seemed to be dangling bottles everywhere and tubes sticking out of him like he was a pincushion. His eye sockets were all shades of black and blue and he had a white bandage around his head. Several ribs had been fractured and they were bandaged up. His arm, too, had been broken in two places. Paul had really done a number on him. He was a mess and I don't think he even knew I was there.

"What's going to happen to Hugh?" Brigitte's eyes when she finally lifted them to mine were huge. But I didn't know that either. I had spoken to his mum at the hospital and she'd sobbed out the words manslaughter and king hit. But that didn't seem right to me. Hugh was defending his brother. These days the media preferred the term coward punch, but that wasn't right, either. Neither Hugh nor Sam were cowards. They were the opposite. Tears pricked my eyes.

"Bridg, I just want us to be friends again. Can we do that? Please."

"I've really missed you, too," said Brigitte, hugging me.

"Mum thinks that I'm going to have to go to court to testify about what happened that night," I whispered. We were all in trouble. It was in the media. It was horrible.

"I have to, too." Brigitte let go of me. "And about the sexual assault charge ... I don't want to think about it now. Are you still coming out with us for my birthday? I don't want to celebrate it. It seems wrong somehow. I mean, how can I? Someone has died because of me. But Mum and the doctor think I should go ahead. Sixteen is apparently a big deal."

"Absolutely." I wiped my nose with my hand and then onto my jeans. It was only then that I noticed what was different about her bed. There were no stuffed toys on it.

"Mum's exchanged the tickets for a play *The 39 Steps*. Have you heard of it?"

I shook my head.

"We had to get extra tickets and it was cheaper that way. Do you think if we asked Sam he'd be up to it? I'm inviting a friend from swim squad."

On the last Saturday night of May, exactly two months after the party, Mr Riley drove Brigitte and me back to the Curtis house. Brigitte sat in the front beside her father and I sat in the back. I was all kinds of nervous about seeing Sam again. Brigitte could tell I was freaking because she didn't talk to me much. Sam and Flynn were waiting in the driveway where the case of beer had once been. Next door, Natasha's house stood dark and quiet. I made room for the boys and they climbed into the back, Sam sitting next to me. I was careful not to touch him. Except for a puckered red scar above his eye, cutting through his eyebrow, he looked the same, but he was quiet and I could tell things were different.

"Happy birthday, Brigitte," he said.

"Did you have a good day?" asked Flynn.

"I had pancakes at a café with Mum *and* Dad, which was super nice, my brother was there, too – not so nice," said Brigitte.

"You should see the loot she got," said Mr Riley.

"Like what?" Flynn said.

"Like an iPad from the best Dad in the world," said Brigitte. She glanced at me appreciatively, "Lucy gave me a really cool bag to carry all my gear when I go to the nationals next year. And I got this." She held up her wrist so we could all see the silver charm in the shape of flippers on a delicate silver chain.

"That's beautiful," I breathed. "Who gave you that?"

"Flynn." Brigitte smiled at him.

Mr Riley dropped us at a Mexican cafe across the road from the theatre in Surry Hills and said he'd be back to pick us up after the play.

We ordered tacos and nachos and margaritas without the tequila, and Brigitte opened her badly wrapped present from Sam. She laughed when she saw what it was: a swimming cap with a shark fin on the top. "I love it," she said, giving him a kiss on the cheek.

"I'm glad," said Sam.

Afterwards, Brigitte and I excused ourselves to go to the toilet. I nudged her. "I can't believe Flynn's present."

She grinned. "I know."

"He is totally into you." I threw my paper towel in the bin. "I had no idea."

Brigitte said, happily, "I know, right?" It was her turn to nudge me.

"How's it going with Sam?"

"Not so well," I said. "But don't worry about me. Tonight is about you."

We sat between the boys and, as the lights dimmed in the theatre, I saw Flynn take Brigitte's hand. I also noticed that Sam had put on his glasses and didn't laugh much even though the play was very funny. Afterwards we waited amongst potted fake palms in the black and white tiled foyer for Mr Riley. Flynn and Brigitte stood to one side, arms entwined, whispering to one another, oblivious to us, the other patrons and the fake palms touching their heads.

"Ah, young love," Sam said, glancing at them.

"Did you know about them?" I jerked my head in their general direction.

"Flynn told me when he came to see me."

"I'm sorry I didn't visit you when you came home. I wanted to, but when I spoke to your mum, she thought it would be best if I gave you some space. Did she tell you that we lost the debate?" With Sam in hospital I was partnered up with another guy, Kai Hung, who forgot a whole point and kept clearing his throat he was so nervous.

"She told me." Sam's face was closed.

"How's Hugh?" I tried again.

"A total mess. Natasha?" Sam was short.

"I wouldn't know."

"You haven't seen her?" His eyes took in mine.

I shook my head.

"Not even at school?"

"She hasn't been there. Has Hugh seen her?"

"Nope. She only lives five metres away and she hasn't bothered to come around once." Sam shook his head. "Times like this, you really find out who your friends are."

"Well, I'm your friend," I said, earnestly and took his hand. He examined our clasped hands.

"I wondered about that," he said.

"I was worried that you blamed me for what happened to Paul. I mean, he was your friend and everything." Sam didn't agree or disagree. I went on, "And then when your mum said that Hugh was going to be charged with manslaughter, I couldn't believe it. It wasn't his fault. Hugh was amazing."

"He pretty much saved my life, Paul was beating the shit outa me." Sam's tone was matter of fact.

"You were pretty amazing, too," I said slowly.

"Yeah, well … We're going to put the house on the market to pay for Hugh's defence counsel. They reckon the manslaughter charge will be dropped to an assault charge because of the circumstances. We'll probably have to leave Northcote Grammar. I don't care, whatever it takes, you know." I stared into his grey troubled eyes. I squeezed his hand harder.

"Yep. Whatever it takes." I looked into his eyes and saw them darken, felt myself go weak. I swallowed. "I want you to know, I'm here for you," and leaned in to kiss him on the cheek.

"Thanks. That means a lot to me." He lowered his gaze to my lips. Time slowed right down but my heart was racing as he leaned over and kissed me on the mouth with slightly parted lips and I sort of lost my breath as if I was on a rollercoaster. I kissed him back and a warmth that started in my stomach soon spread out all the way down to my knees. And if his arms hadn't been around my waist and my hands at his neck, I might have fallen from the intensity of these feelings. I closed my eyes until there was nothing in the world but this kiss. I wanted it to go on forever. I could feel his hands move along the curve of my hips, bringing us closer still, like he couldn't get enough of me.

"Lucy?" he whispered into my mouth. "We need to clear something up."

"Huh?" I was slow to come out of it. I opened my eyes, pulling away. He didn't let me go too far.

"Can this be called a first date if neither of us paid?" he asked. His arms were warm around me.

"We'll have to go out again just so one of us can pay," I said, leaning in again.

He touched my forehead with his lips, "That's what I thought, too."